Small Town, Big Secrets

A Trinity River Romance

Elsie Davis

Cover Design by getcovers.com

Edited by Stacy Abrams and Lydia Sharp

Edited by Elaine Hyatt (Clarity Editing Services-2024)

Sweet Romance Publishing

Sweetromancepublishing.com

PO Box 778

Liberty, NC 27298

To all my readers who fell in love with Kayla and Dylan in Back in the Rancher's Arms. Many of you took the time to let me know what you wanted to read next, so here it is— Becky's story.
Hope you enjoy!
Amos 5:24
But let justice roll on like a river, righteousness like a never-failing stream!

To all my readers who fell in love with Kayla and Dylan in Back in the Rancher's Arms. Many of you took the time to let me know what you wanted to read next, so here it is— Becky's story.
Hope you enjoy!
Amos 5:24
But let justice roll on like a river, righteousness like a never-failing stream!

Chapter One

♥

Becky walked out of the doctor's office, the blast of Texas heat hitting her hard, but not as hard as the news she'd just received. Twelve thousand dollars. The deductible and copay on Byron's hernia surgery were far more than she'd ever expected. In hindsight, the lowest-cost insurance plan might not have been such a good idea, but it had been all she could afford. Of course, there also was no way she could have ever foreseen her five-year-old son needing to be hospitalized for surgery. No number of fundraisers the town did for her would raise this kind of money.

She pulled her long hair back off to one side of her head and rubbed her neck, wiping the pool of sweat that had formed there. Becky already worked full-time at Charlie's Bar and Grill, and her mother worked full-time at the Parker mansion. Between the two of them, they barely managed their expenses, but neither one could take on a second job, at least not while they had to juggle Byron's care. Her sister was a big help, but she and her mom agreed Julia's studies came first.

There was one other avenue she hadn't pursued, but considering the magnitude of the copay, Becky wasn't left with much choice. For her son, she'd do anything—and that included asking Byron's father.

Not that she expected the miserable cur to help, but she would ask.

The weasel hadn't even acknowledged his own son. Instead, he'd gone out of his way to make sure no one knew he was connected to the boy in any way, forcing Becky into silence.

She glanced at her watch. *Darn it.* The conversation with the financial administrator had taken longer than she'd planned, and now she was late for work. Becky hurried down the sidewalk toward Charlie's. The last thing she needed was to lose her job, especially with Ethan considering her for an assistant manager's position. He was a great boss and a good friend, but to him, his restaurant had to come first, something she understood.

Becky reached into her purse and pulled out the baggie with her peanut butter and jelly sandwich she'd fixed for herself this morning. No such thing as a leisurely lunch today. She pulled out the first half, the sticky red jelly coming out the sides and getting all over her fingers. She licked the outer edges to catch the strawberry goo before it dripped onto her clothes.

She reached for the napkin tucked in the front pocket of her purse and yanked it out, but in doing so, the papers from the doctor's office she'd shoved in there earlier came out with the napkin and fell to the ground. Sandwich in one hand, she juggled her purse and stooped down to grab the papers. Her day couldn't get any worse.

She stood and rounded the corner, colliding with the hulking chest of a man, her sandwich firmly smushed between them. The man's arms came around her, preventing her from falling.

Apparently, her day *could* get worse.

"I'm so sorry." Becky stepped back, getting her first good look at the guy she'd broadsided.

"Are you okay?" Mr. Business Executive asked, letting his hands drop when he realized she wasn't in danger of falling flat on her face.

Of course it had to be a guy who looked like he belonged on the cover of a magazine. Dark, wavy hair that was cut in a roguish style and brushed off to the side. His olive complexion had nothing to do with the sun. Chocolate brown eyes, a cleanly shaven face, and a strong jaw completed the picture. Swoon worthy.

But there was nothing swoon worthy about the peanut butter and jelly now plastered across his suit coat, shirt, and tie. This was a day she clearly should have stayed in bed. And considering the man's frown as he gazed down at the mess she'd made of his clothes, he would agree.

"I'm fine. I'm so sorry. Here, let me help." Using her napkin, she began to wipe at his shirt. Each stroke only smeared the gooey mixture worse, turning his blue shirt an ugly brownish-red color, making him smell like he'd plastered peanut butter on as aftershave this morning.

The man reached up to grasp her hand, stopping her from doing any more damage than she'd already done. "I'm not sure that's helping," he said with a laugh.

His smile reached his eyes, the corners crinkling. Way better than a frown.

Becky was mesmerized for just a moment, lost in the kindness of his expression. Most people would've been furious with her, but not this guy. "I feel awful."

"Where were you in such a hurry to go? Or do you just make a habit of meeting people in unorthodox ways?" The warm sound of his laugh was pleasing, his joke at a time like this catching her off guard.

"My job," she said. "And this isn't good. I can't be late— or any later than I already am. I've really got to run. Is there anything I can do to make this up to you?"

"I'll get it handled. Don't worry. I'd hate for you to be late for work." The man removed his suit coat.

"Are you sure? I could go get some water and more napkins..." She'd been late far too often trying to manage Byron's care and doctor visits, but she didn't feel right leaving him like this.

"I'm sure."

Becky exhaled, her breath coming out as one big *whoosh*. "Thank you for being so understanding." She turned to leave, but then she paused, half twisting back around. "And no, I don't make a habit of bumping into people, for the record."

"I'm glad to hear it. I won't have to keep an eye out for you while I'm in town."

His laughter continued to ring in her ears as she hurried down the sidewalk, stopping only to toss the rest of her sandwich in the trash can on the corner.

She pushed open the front door of the restaurant, and the overhead bill jingled, announcing her arrival. Ethan looked up from the bar then glanced down at his watch.

"Sorry I'm late. The meeting at the doctor's office ran over." Becky raced across the room toward the back kitchen doors.

"Slow down. I know you've been late a lot, but I also understand why, and it's okay. I consider us friends, and I'm a reasonable man." Ethan was more than reasonable, but it didn't mean she should take advantage of him.

She stopped at the end of the bar. "I also know there are at least twenty people here in Riverbend waiting to take my place if you ever become not okay with it."

"So how did it go?" Ethan slid a glass of beer across the counter to one of the lunch customers.

Life had taught Becky to keep her affairs private, and she wasn't about to change that now, no matter how desperate she was feeling. "It wasn't good. It's going to cost more than I expected, but I'll figure it out. Mom and I always do." It was the truth, but this time, she wasn't so sure.

"I know how determined you can be—and how hard-working. I'll let you get to it. You've got your normal section today." Ethan went back to wiping down the countertop.

Becky grabbed her apron hanging on the hook in the hallway that led to the kitchen and tied it behind her back, letting out a sigh of relief. It was just another day in the long line of many to come. Not at all like the dream she had growing up, back when she had big plans to leave Riverbend and head for the city. Before she'd fallen for Jack Parker's lies, thinking she was different and that he loved her.

Boy, had she been wrong. It was a mistake she would pay for over and over, but one she couldn't completely regret. Becky loved her son, no matter the circumstances surrounding his birth.

Jack had been more concerned about his football scholarship to Houston University than about his son, which was why he threatened to have her mother fired for stealing if Becky revealed his identity to anyone. She was the housekeeper for the Parkers, so his threats had been quite effective, just as he'd known they would be.

Unfortunately, staying off Jack's radar and out of the limelight would no longer be an option. He was her last hope to get the money needed for Byron's surgery.

She could only hope time would've matured him, or at least made him a more reasonable man. She also hoped the self-control she'd learned over the years would keep her in good stead when dealing with him, because there was a lot at stake.

Time had changed her in other ways. Seeing the community pull together to help her with Byron...their outpouring of love and support was nothing short of amazing. Becky finally understood the feeling of belonging, and the last thing she wanted to do was uproot her family and leave. Once upon a time, it had been her dream, but not anymore.

But leaving was exactly what would need to happen if Jack made trouble for her and her mother, because employment and town sentiment would turn against them if the Parkers set their mind to turn them into outcasts. They were that powerful.

Chapter Two

♥

Steve stared after the woman as she walked away, realizing a little belatedly he was just as much to blame for their collision as she might've been. He hated for her to think it was all her fault, but his dad's text had come through at just that moment, and like every other person in America, he'd made the mistake of not stopping to read it.

The Judge cancelling their lunch appointment with no definite reschedule time hadn't surprised Steve. In fact, it would have surprised him more if his father had actually shown up at Charlie's Bar and Grill.

There were two reasons Steve had come to town. One, to meet with his dad and question him about some of the rumors more than a few people had secretly brought to his attention. And two, a private meeting with the Cattlemen's Association. His father's cancelation didn't change the fact that he needed to eat lunch. A quick stop at his car to drop off his briefcase and he'd head for Charlie's Bar and Grill, one of the only restaurants in town. If he remembered correctly, the food there was fairly decent.

Not that he'd been around much since he'd left for college. Houston was more his style, and it was the most direct route to what he wanted most in life—to become the youngest judge elected in the state of Texas. Someone not tainted by politics. Someone able to represent people who couldn't speak for themselves and needed an advocate. Of course, the bonus came from the fact he'd beat out his father to the D.A. position if he won this election—a record his father currently held.

He looked down at his ruined tie. His dry cleaner might be able to salvage the shirt and suit coat, but until he got back to his mother's house, he was stuck looking like he just had lunch with a two year old. Although the actual culprit was a very beautiful woman, and he found it quite easy to forgive her.

It was probably for the better his dad had canceled, because now he wouldn't have to listen to him make comments about his sloppy attire. The man had always been a perfectionist with anything related to his career—just nothing related to his family or his marriage.

Steve entered Charlie's, the bell on the door announcing his arrival. Red and white checked tablecloths covered a dozen or so tables and the barstools at the bar, high tops with matching red vinyl. The place hadn't changed much over the years, including the worn wood floors. He wasn't sure if it was for the ambiance or just too expensive to redo. The patio outside, however, was a new addition.

"Welcome to Charlie's. Sit wherever you'd like," the server behind the counter called out, raising her voice above the din of the patrons and jukebox playing a country song.

Steve waved at her to indicate he understood and made his way toward a table in the back corner. He picked the seat that faced the outdoors window, preferring to observe things going on around him. Details were always good, and he never knew what he'd learn just by watching.

Off to the side, a server started toward him. He looked up, surprised to find the peanut butter and jelly lady, her blonde hair pulled back into a ponytail now, but her green eyes not a vision he'd forget anytime soon. The color reminded him of jade. The apron she wore covered up most of the curvy figure he'd noticed earlier.

Her smile faded as she reached the table, equally recognizing him. "We meet again. But hopefully under better circumstances. Welcome to Charlie's."

"Should I run now, or have you reached your limit of disasters for the day?" He chuckled.

"You should be safe. Don't think I've seen you in here before, and I've worked for Ethan for a couple of years now. Not from around this neck of the woods, are you?" The server handed him his menu, her inquisitive glance all too obvious. But then, everyone in Riverbend thought they had a right to know his business. It was one of the reasons he'd left as soon as he graduated high school.

"Houston. I live in Houston," he qualified. Technically, he was from around here, but it wasn't the place he claimed as home. Riverbend belonged to his father—Tumble County's judge.

"I see. And from your attire, I assume you're here on business. Are you meeting someone for lunch?" She glanced toward the door.

"Not anymore." He shrugged.

"Well, in that case, I won't set another place. Charlie's has a lot of great food, but if you're looking for recommendations, the beef stew is known as some of the best in the county. Another great option is the cheesy chicken pot pie, and it's on special for lunch today. While you decide, what can I get you to drink?" She rolled off his options.

"Sweet tea would be nice. As long as it doesn't end up on my lap." He couldn't help but tease her. He was glad he'd run into her, because it would give him a chance to apologize.

"You're not going to let that go, are you?" She grinned, hands on her hips in mock frustration.

"Probably not until I get a chance to change." Steve glanced at her name tag. "Name's Steve, by the way. Nice to meet you, Becky." He held out his hand, eager to meet her on more than a server-patron basis, his interest piqued by the woman whose smile made him feel warm and welcome. Something he didn't normally experience the few times he'd come into town to see his mother. It was surprising he hadn't run into her before, but he'd never forget her beautiful face now that he'd met her.

"I'll take an order of the beef stew," he said. "And while I'm waiting, I'm going to step into the men's room and try to clean up a little. I had a mishap with a PB&J lady earlier today."

She held up her hands in mock exasperation and shook her head.

Steve made his way toward the hall that led to the back and the kitchens, the smell of garlic making him realize how hungry he was. Grabbing a couple of paper towels, he wet them and started to wipe away what was left of the peanut butter and jelly, but the oils had already soaked in and no amount of rubbing, or soap was going to help at this point.

He returned to his seat and slid into the booth. Becky had already brought his drink and a basket of bread. It wasn't long before the order-up bell clanged from the direction of the kitchen. She returned, beef stew in hand and a ready smile on her face.

"It doesn't look like washing did you much good. Again, I'm sorry. I don't think you should leave me a tip today, in all fairness. You can use it toward getting the stains out."

"Since you're being all fair and everything, I should probably tell you I was equally to blame. I was reading a text when I came around the corner. The lunch cancelation. I think your tip is safe." If anything, her tip percentage had just gone higher, her sense of honesty and fairness something he appreciated in people.

Becky breathed a sigh of relief, her smile genuine. "Then enjoy your lunch. And let me know if there's anything else I can get you." She turned to walk away.

"There is one thing," he said.

She stopped and turned back, a questioning look on her face.

"The place seems to be clearing out, and if you get a few minutes, maybe you'd like to join me. Save a guy from having to eat alone with no one to talk to." Totally out of character for him to request such a thing, but also totally something he couldn't resist asking, her open friendliness calling to him, making him want to know more.

"I'm sure that's not a problem you have regularly." She winked, her teasing taking him by surprise.

"You said to let you know, so that's what I'm doing." Her comment left him wondering if he wasn't the only one interested in getting to know her more.

"Haha, funny guy. I'll see what I can do, but don't hold your breath." She turned and sashayed away, and Steve admired the gentle sway of her hips.

Becky had a winning smile for every customer she waited on. It was only when he noticed a young girl enter the restaurant that her smile slipped. Which made no sense at all, since the girl was the spitting image of Becky. His guess would be a younger sister.

The two talked, Becky shaking her head at whatever the girl was trying to tell her. Minutes later, he noticed Becky pulling her tips from the pocket of her apron, counting out the dollars one by one, and then handing them to the girl. There was something about the stilted action that made him stop and wonder more about his server. Her entire demeanor had changed in a split second, the lines of stress evident on her face. There was a story, but not one she'd likely share with him. He'd do well to mind his own business, only do what he came to town for, and get back to Houston.

It wasn't like he didn't have enough to do already, the pressures of the campaign heating up and taking more and more of his time. He loved law, but the public scrutiny of his life—not so much. And regarding his campaign manager's strong suggestion he find a "love at first sight" romance and a bride to improve his poll ratings, well, that simply went too far. Not only did he never want to marry, but add to that the issue of finding a woman to fit the bill, and the entire idea became ludicrous.

Steve could only hope his popularity went up on its own, based more on his record than his marital status. Harry had practically shoved him out of the office, claiming he needed to spend less time in there and more time out with people. What he preferred was to be left alone to do his job to the best of his abilities.

His own personal crusade against dead-beat dads, or DBDs as he called them, was proof of the success he found from the dedication to his job. It was just one of many areas he targeted and what he wanted the constituents to think about when they went to the polls.

When the most recent complaint from the Cattleman's Association had landed on his desk for review, Steve had made it a priority to do some behind-the-scenes poking around. The lead investigator's request for him to talk to the judge about it gave Steve the perfect cover to investigate the charge of unfair practices being used to foreclose on local ranchers' and farmers' properties. Coincidence or not, he wasn't sure, but the proposed changes to existing laws would make it difficult for the ranchers in Texas to get access to water rights during times of drought.

The whole situation reeked of political interference and big business opportunities, and where corruption could be found, his own father, Tumble County's judge, wouldn't be far away. Never quite doing anything illegal, but typically right in the thick of it.

Figuring out what was going on and putting an end to it would go a long way toward improving his public image. But it was more than that for Steve. The two-year drought had been tough on people across Texas, and the idea that someone or some entity was trying to take unfair advantage rankled him.

As the potential future district attorney, it was his job to protect them.

Becky returned to his table to check on him, her smile and positive attitude firmly back in place. She was a true professional, completely able to separate personal things from business. "Is everything okay?" She placed his bill face-down on the table.

"Other than the fact you're too busy and don't have time to sit and chat, I'm good." He winked.

"Oh..." Her brow wrinkled. "I didn't think you were serious."

"Dead serious. How else am I supposed to ask you to have lunch with me?"

"Now, I know you're joking. Having fun at my expense." She shook her head and frowned.

"No, I'm very serious. I'm only in town a few days and would love the chance to get to know you more." It was the truth, shocking even himself, but true.

"Why? Big city slicker like you. I can't imagine you'd want to take out a country mouse."

"You're far from being a country mouse, trust me. Give me ten minutes of your time to get to know me and then you can make a decision. No pressure. I'll even buy you lunch, seeing as I'm partly responsible you didn't get to eat yours."

"I think I can handle that. I'm not against a free meal— just relationships," she said, scrunching up her nose. "Let me see if I can get Katie to cover my customers for a few minutes and I'll be back."

She packed a lot of information in one small sentence. He was relieved to hear she wasn't into relationships, because that certainly wasn't what he was after, either. There was no place in his life for things like that. It made the two of them all the more a good match for a simple date, something to pass an evening away while in town.

Steve was pleased when she returned with a burger and fries and then slid into the booth seat across from him.

She sat down and took a bite of her burger, not at all shy about eating in front of him.

"Was that your sister I saw you talking to earlier?" Family was always a good place to start.

"Pretty observant of you. I wasn't aware you were watching. But yes, that was my younger sister, Julia. She had big ideas of joining her friends at the soda shop down the street, another place you should try out while you're in town. They have awesome banana splits, with a scoop of strawberry, vanilla, and chocolate ice cream, all drizzled with pineapple and chocolate and strawberry sauce, and then topped with whipped cream and nuts. I'm craving it now just talking about them. I haven't had one in forever."

"Well, there you have it." Steve leaned back, positive she'd just given him his ticket to a date.

"Have what?"

"The answer to you saying yes. I'll treat you to a banana split." He grinned. "How non-relationship is that? Just two friends sharing dessert."

"And when did we become friends?" Her grin took the edge off the words.

"I'm thinking it started right about the time you smashed into me with your peanut butter and jelly sandwich." He chuckled, knowing he had her.

"Indeed." She smiled. "So, what do you do, Peanut Butter Man?"

"I'm an attorney."

"Oh, good grief. No wonder you're into details. Are you in town for any particular purpose? Are you handling a case for someone locally?" Becky leaned forward, her interest appearing genuine.

"Now who's looking for details?" he teased. "But the simple answer to your question is no, I'm not handling a case. I'm just here checking out a few things." It was more than he should have said, but he wouldn't lie.

"Like?" She pressed for more.

"I'd rather not say. Word travels fast in a small town."

"True." Becky shifted in her seat, her gaze focused on the french fries she was pushing around on her plate haphazardly with a fork. Stopping, she looked up at him. "Since you don't want to talk about what you're doing in town, then maybe you can answer a different question. A law question."

The earlier smile had slipped from her face, Becky turning serious on him. The sudden change in her demeanor caught him by surprise.

"Ask away. Feel free to pick my brain, as long as it's not related to any case I'm working on, and I'll be happy to answer."

"It's for a friend of mine. But she's having trouble with her—her child's father." Becky tripped over the words, a clear indicator she likely was talking about herself.

He leaned forward, encouraging her to confide, and Steve found himself wanting to help her in any way he could. "Go on."

"Well, I was just wondering how the law looked at a parent who was never around and then suddenly pops up wanting custody. Would a court ever side with an absentee parent like that?" Becky's intensity as she asked the question confirmed his suspicions—she was talking about something far more personal than a friend's problems.

Perhaps her sister's father was back in town and making trouble? There was no clear-cut answer because the details would make a case either for or against the allegations and request, but he could give her the generalities. Anything to help put her at ease.

"In general, the absentee parent might be able to prove a good reason they were absent and gain visitation, but it would be rare to gain full custody unless they could prove they were never told about the child. More so if that person could prove the current custodial parent was not a good parent."

"But it *is* still possible?"

"Possible, but not probable. Not generally speaking. The other thing that can happen is a paternity test to prove parentage and, with that, an order for child support to help your friend financially. Children are expensive." The look of relief on her face was clear. Whether about the person getting custody or the part about child support, he wasn't sure.

"Tell me about it." Becky's gaze drifted off to watch another table. Her slip was more revealing than she knew.

She looked back at him. "But thanks. I feel better—for my friend, that is." She leaned back in the booth, the tension ebbing from her shoulders as she took a deep breath. "I probably should get back to work. And to answer your question, yes, I'll join you for a banana split. Is tomorrow okay? Around two?"

It would give him a chance to do some poking around first, which was why he was in town in the first place. "Two o'clock is perfect."

Becky slid out of the booth then turned back to him. "Thanks for the advice. Keep the tip and count it as payment for the information. You can settle up at the register."

"Thanks for saying yes, Becky." Steve realized he meant it. He was looking forward to seeing her again tomorrow. He was also glad she hadn't recognized him as a Parker, and he'd done all he could not to name drop, preferring she didn't make the connection. Not yet, anyway. He was guessing she was at least seven or eight years younger than him, which explained why they'd never crossed paths when he was in school.

Over ice cream, he'd tell her, but by then, he hoped to secure her acceptance of a dinner invitation. He watched as another customer checked out at the register and then proceeded to stuff change in a jar on the counter. Becky's smile was genuine and appreciative.

She had no way of knowing Steve's focused efforts on DBDs or the personal reason he'd made them a priority. His childhood friend Winston and his family didn't have an advocate when they needed one, and since getting into law, Steve had worked to change the system. His goal was to provide more assistance to the single mothers left with the responsibility of raising a child on their own.

Steve had tried to make things better for Winston, but he'd failed. Or, rather, the system had failed, and his father had even taken a part in the devastation to the Roberts family. Steve rubbed his forefinger across the scar above his right eye, the one he got protecting Winston from a bully.

He never saw Winston again after social services stepped in and put him in foster care, claiming the mother was unfit to care for her two children. Even then, Steve recognized the power the Judge held. What stung worse was that his father had sided with the bully's parents, taking their word over Steve's.

Steve vowed back then that one day he'd have that power but that he'd use it for good.

He stood to leave, tossing a hundred-dollar bill on the table. Maybe Becky's sister could get an ice cream, too.

The other server rang up his bill, and he paid with cash. He glanced down at the plastic jar next to the register to see who needed help. To his surprise, it was a picture of Becky taped to the front. Becky and a young boy with the caption "Byron needs your help." *Her son?*

Now, more than ever, he knew the questions she'd asked were for herself, not a friend. She had a son, and by the looks of it, her son had a DBD. She was worried about the jerk stepping in and taking custody from her. Steve glanced around, noticing Becky on the other side of the restaurant. He opened his wallet and pulled another hundred out then stuffed it into the jar.

Chapter Three

♥

BECKY SPENT THE EARLY morning trying to clean up the small house she and her family lived in, using the time Byron slept to her advantage. The house was old and run down, but it didn't mean they couldn't do their best to make it look nice inside. Outside was another story. But it wasn't their house, and she and her mom couldn't afford the paint, much less pay someone to paint it. Or have it landscaped. Or fix any of the number of things that needed fixing.

Folks from their church had come over once before to chip in and help clean up the yard, but time had a way of erasing their gracious efforts. And the homeowner had made it clear they didn't have the money to fix the place up, reminding her often they'd rented the house "as is" if Becky asked for anything to be done. She was grateful they had a roof over their heads, though. Even if it did leak at times.

"Julia," Becky said to her sister, "Mom just left for your parent-teacher conference this morning, and I've got to run an errand. Can you watch Byron, since you don't have school today?" Her mother's absence from work at the mansion, where she was part of the house staff, was exactly the window of opportunity Becky needed to visit the place. The last thing she wanted to do was raise her mother's suspicions regarding the up until now unknown identity of Byron's father. Not even Kayla, her best friend, knew the truth.

"Sure, I can watch him. When's the little bug going to wake up?" Julia laughed.

"Soon. I should be back within the hour. Thanks." Becky had gone over every possibility, but seeing no other option, she decided she had to talk to Jack. Beg him to help pay for his son's surgery. Steve's advice gave her the confidence she needed. The NFL wannabe's threats against her mother were a definite consideration still, but the threat of losing Byron to Jack's powerful parents was infinitely worse. Becky knew she'd been a good mother, and for her son's sake, she was willing to risk Jack's anger by approaching him to ask for the money.

At this point, the worst he could do was say no. It wasn't like she was revealing his identity to any-one—she just needed his money. And it was only right that he help, anyway.

"Just make sure he eats his breakfast and brushes his teeth. And if you go out back to play, make sure he's got a warm enough sweater on. It's a little cool this morning."

"Just go, will you? I'm sixteen, not eleven. I know how to take care of Byron."

"Okay. You're right." It was hard to believe her little sister was so grown up. It wouldn't be long before she'd be graduating high school. And, with any luck, off to college. Her whole life was ahead of her, and the last thing she wanted Julia to do was mess it up the way Becky had. Julia was just starting to get the boy craze, and Becky had vowed to keep a close eye on her.

She grabbed her purse and headed out the door, trying to calm her nerves, which wasn't an easy thing to do. As she drove toward the Parker mansion, her fingers gripped the steering wheel, and she played out what she would say to Jack. But asking an absentee dad for money wasn't an easy thing to put into words, knowing every one had to count. Failure wasn't an option. Somehow, she had to appeal to his sense of decency, if there was any in him.

Her thoughts drifted to Steve. Yes, he'd helped her, but then he'd also managed to completely confuse her. He seemed friendly enough, and Becky didn't have a lot of time for friends. She didn't normally respond to customers flirting, but it had helped her to focus on something other than Byron's surgery and the absurd amount of money it cost. Customers generally weren't interested in her personal woes, and anything less than a positive attitude at work usually meant lower tips. But the opportunity for free legal advice wasn't one that would fall into her lap again. She couldn't just let it go.

His invitation to take her for ice cream had come as a surprise and, as it turned out, was a treat she couldn't resist. At the time, accepting his offer seemed like a great idea. A no-strings-attached ice cream date. Something completely innocent. But then he'd gone and left her an oversize tip. *Twice.*

The whole town knew about her situation, well-meaning folk all too quick to set up fundraisers to help. For some reason, though, the fact Steve knew of her troubles bothered her. Especially since he'd tossed his money around like it was nothing. Just like Jack and the rest of the Parker family. Not that she wasn't grateful for Steve's money, but she had zero interest in money-driven people. She wasn't sure what to think of their upcoming date anymore. How could she even look at him now without seeing dollar signs?

Becky drove through town, and it wasn't long before she was on the outskirts of Riverbend. She turned into the Parkers' driveway, passing through the open wrought-iron gate and followed the paved road to their mansion, stopping in front. Her old rusty Toyota looked severely out of place, but she didn't work for the wealthy family and had no intention of parking in the back like she was one of the employees.

Becky hoped that by arriving this early, Jack would still be home. She took a deep breath, hoping that somehow, she could convince Jack to help his son. Sliding out of the car before she chickened out, she made her way up the grand staircase that led to the double wooden doors. She lifted the wrought-iron ring of the door knocker and tapped it against the metal plate several times. Becky shifted from side to side, the rocking motion something she'd never gotten rid of after Byron was born and spending many long nights rocking him to sleep. The motion was oddly comforting to her, especially when she felt anxious or stressed.

Finally, the door opened, and a uniformed butler stood before her—cold and impersonal, his back ramrod straight. His gaze flicked briefly toward her car and then back at her. "May I help you?" he asked, his voice laced with disdain.

"I'd like to speak with Jack Parker, please." She tried to speak up and show confidence, but her attempt was a failure, her voice coming out dismally low and soft.

"Mr. Jack Parker is not in residence. And I'm certain you have no appointment with him, as his schedule is clear. Good day, madam." The butler started to shut the door, dismissing her out of hand.

Try harder. This is for Byron. "Wait!" She held up her hand to stop the door from closing and took a step forward. "Please. Can you tell me where to find him? It's important." She hated the tremble in her voice, but this was her last hope.

"I would not be at liberty to inform you of his whereabouts. I suggest you make an appointment to see him. It's the best I can do to help you." The butler's demeanor had changed ever so slightly, a hint of compassion in his eyes, but it did nothing to soften his words. Perhaps he, too, was not a fan of Jack's, but his job depended on him being professional. She'd probably get nothing out of him.

"Thank you. Do you have his phone number or a way for me to contact him?"

"No, I'm sorry. I'm not at liberty to give out that information."

Just as she suspected.

"What's going on down here, Philip?" a vaguely familiar voice called out from somewhere inside.

"A visitor for Jack, sir. It's under control," the butler quickly assured whoever had spoken. "She wants his phone number, and I've assured her it's not possible for me to give that information out."

"I'll handle this, Philip. If you could let Roberta know I'm ready for breakfast, that would be great. Thank you."

Becky tried to peer around the butler but still couldn't see the man who'd joined them.

"As you wish, sir." Philip turned and walked away.

The door was opened wide, and suddenly she was face-to-face with...Steve?

"What are you doing here?" she blurted.

"Becky? I live here. I mean, my family lives here, and I'm staying with them while I'm in town." He shook his head as if baffled. "The better question is what are *you* doing here?"

He lived there. He had money. Steve, as in Steve *Parker*. As in Jack's older brother.

No. No. No. This was *not* good. Why hadn't she made the connection sooner?

"I needed to talk. To Jack," she clarified. It wasn't like he didn't know why she was here, the butler having clued him in.

"So, Philip didn't misspeak? You're here to see Jack and not me?" Steve frowned as if the information didn't sit well with him at all.

"Yes, I'm sorry." She shrugged, unsure of what else she could say.

"Interesting and disappointing, to say the least." It was like a wall had been erected in the space of seconds, yesterday's friendliness between them a thing of the past.

"Jack and I are...friends. I didn't realize you were his brother. I need to talk to him, but your butler couldn't tell me how to find him. Can you?" She'd come this far, and she had to keep trying for Byron's sake.

"If you were friends, you'd know he's been out of town for a few weeks and isn't expected back anytime soon." The cool and aloof tone of his voice signaled the end of the discussion.

The intensity of the moment hit her hard. She'd run into a brick wall. There was no way to get the money now, and Byron wouldn't have the surgery. Prayer was all she had left that nothing would rupture and cause her son complications. The possibility he could die was more than she could bear.

Becky started to shake, her emotions uncontrollable. Tears filled her eyes and ran down unchecked as she turned away. She stumbled down the step, grateful when Steve caught her, preventing her from tumbling to the bottom in a heap.

"Why do you need my brother?" His gaze was intense and demanding.

"I told you, we're friends." Archenemies was more like it, but she could never tell Steve the truth. Jack's threats loomed over her like a black shadow and forced her to remain silent.

"I see." Steve nodded. "Wait right here." He turned and went back inside, returning moments later and handing her a piece of paper.

Becky glanced down and saw Jack's name and number. She let out a sigh of relief, tears threatening to spill over. "Thank you."

"You look like you need a friend." It was all he said by way of explanation.

There'd be no banana split for her today, the pitying look on Steve's face a clear message. Not that she would go, anyway. Jack's brother was off-limits in more ways than she could count.

Chapter Four

♥

STEVE WATCHED AS BECKY drove away, her blue car looking like it had seen better days. He shook his head, still unable to believe the woman he couldn't stop thinking about last night was more than likely one of Jack's past transgressions. Although, judging from what he'd heard, there were plenty of those to go around.

Giving Becky his number was crossing the line when it came to the unspoken code between brothers, but then being seven years older than Jack had never left them close—especially after his parent's divorce.

Becky's tears had been his undoing.

He didn't buy the friend story. Jack didn't have women friends, and if he did, they certainly wouldn't be reduced to tears simply because he was out of town. What he couldn't understand was why a woman like Becky would be interested in a guy like his brother. He would have thought her smarter than that. Question was, how current was the *friendship*? Her word choice, not his.

The more he thought about it, the more he started putting together options. Options he didn't like but very real possibilities. Becky's questions about paternity laws, and her need for money for her son's surgery, and then her magical appearance at the Parker mansion, looking for Jack instead of him. They were all signs that pointed in one direction. Was Byron Jack's son? And if he was, why had Steve never heard about him? Was it possible he was an uncle?

One thing that was for certain, however, was Becky's surprise to find him in residence. She really hadn't known who he was, and the thought gave him some comfort.

Steve was determined to get answers to his questions, but in the meantime, he'd let Jack handle his own mess when it came to Becky and whatever she needed from him. Jack was too much like their father, a favorite with the ladies but low on commitment. But unlike his father, Jack hadn't married the girl he got pregnant. Worse still, he hadn't claimed the boy as his son.

His father might be a selfish jerk, but if Steve's suspicions were right, Jack was worse. Much worse.

There was always the possibility he was way off base, but his gut told him differently.

It was either that or Becky was a gold-digger. He wasn't a betting man, but if he was, his odds were on Jack as a DBD. His brother wasn't exactly a stand-up guy.

Steve went back into the house to get his breakfast, surprised to discover his mother beat him there. She wasn't much of a breakfast person or a morning person in general. "Good morning, Mother."

"Good morning." Impeccably dressed and not a hair out of place, his mother reached for her teacup, her hand weighed down by rings set with stones that all but shouted her wealth to everyone she met. In case one couldn't tell by her clothes and fancy up-do or the chauffeur who drove her around in a Rolls Royce through what some called a two- horse town.

"What brings you to the breakfast table, Mother?"

"Do I need a reason to talk to my son? It's not like you come to see me often, so I'm sure there's a reason for your visit. I'm just not one to sit around and wait on you to find the time to tell me." His mother knew him well.

"Actually, I'm in town to talk to the Judge. He canceled on me yesterday, but I'm hoping to meet up with him later. I've got to get back to Houston. My campaign is ramping up, and the face of the election is missing in action."

"What's so important with your father?" She looked at him, suspicion in her eyes. He wasn't his father, but after the divorce, his mother found it difficult to trust anyone. Not that he blamed her. Olivia Parker always got straight to the point, one of the few things they had in common.

"It's a business matter. There are some grumblings coming from the Cattleman's Association, and I'm just looking to see what the Judge may or may not have heard. It's a sensitive subject and one that requires handling in person."

There was a lot more to it than that, but it wasn't information he intended to share. Riverbend was a small town, and the bridge club she frequented consisted of nothing more than a group of old biddy gossipy women that sat around talking about others during their frequent social hour.

"I see." She took a dainty sip from her teacup. "It would be nice if you came to Hallbrook once in a while."

"I'm busy, Mother." He shrugged. She should understand that his work came first. It was the lesson his father had taught him well.

"The other women in our club are always flaunting their children's visits. Imagine how it looks when I have two sons who never bother to visit."

"Perhaps you should be having this conversation with Jack. He's the one living off your good graces. He should have plenty of time to play the patronizing son." Steve couldn't keep the derision out of his voice. His brother was never a good topic, now more than ever.

"How long are you in town for?"

"Too long." Long enough to hopefully get some leads on who was targeting Tumble County landowners and foreclosing on their properties. There were too many in a concentrated area to be considered a coincidence.

"Hopefully, that's long enough for me to show you off, prove I really do have a son." She jutted her chin upward, matching the haughty expression on her face. "Now, if you'll excuse me, the ladies are waiting for me at the bridge club." His mother gave him one of her infamous stiff-air hugs and then left. Hopefully, he'd be long gone before she had the chance to parade him around town like a prized pet.

Steve spent the rest of the day talking to a couple of the landowners personally, trying to find out their story. His expertise in ferreting out information might lead him to the root of the problem, but it would do nothing to save the landowners already caught up in an unfair situation.

Of course, in the middle of all that, he'd shown up at the ice cream shop just to confirm his suspicions Becky would be a no-show. Her absence proved him right. He still hadn't gotten over the shock of her showing up at the mansion and asking for his brother, the whole scene not sitting well with him.

The image of her face as tears rolled down her cheeks never far away, the day went by unbearably slow, the evening worse. Becky might be his brother's problem, but his desire to protect the underdog was strong.

But that's where his interest had to end.

The next morning, Steve poured a cup of coffee and stared out across the back forty. Acres and acres of land that belonged to his mother, acreage she didn't use. The tall grasses waved gracefully as the wind gusted. Whoever was buying up land wouldn't come after anything the Parkers owned, but no one else was safe. Some of the families had been on their properties for generations, and it was wrong for someone to take unfair advantage of them for financial gain.

His phone rang, and he picked up the call. "Hey, Eric, what's up?" His best friend had been gone the past two weeks, on his honeymoon of all things. Something Steve hadn't been able to talk him out of doing when he first got engaged. Not that he hadn't tried.

"Just checking in to let you know I survived the honeymoon." Eric laughed. "All your dire warnings have yet to materialize." His laughter only grew louder.

"Give it time. Or maybe you'll be one of the lucky ones. I hope so for your sake. And Jen's a great girl." He meant it. His friend had found a wonderful woman, and he truly hoped they proved him wrong. The last thing he wanted for Eric was for him to go through what he'd witnessed growing up.

"Rome was amazing, but it's good to be back in Texas. I'm ready to get things in order and on schedule." Once upon a time, Eric had been a workaholic, but Jen had put her foot down, demanding he learn to balance his work with his personal life. His friend was still working on it but was well on his way to accomplishing just that.

"Two weeks away will be tough to catch up. But if anyone can do it, it'll be you."

"That's because I'm willing to delegate, unlike you, who always has to control every last detail of the case."

"That's true, but only because Jen made you learn. Unlike me, which is why I'm in Riverbend." Although the things he needed to accomplish here weren't exactly anything he could delegate to someone else.

"Riverbend? I thought you hated that place." Eric was surprised, but no more so than he'd been when he decided to make the trip.

"I do, but business brought me here. I'm working on some leads for the Cattlemen's Association. They filed a complaint citing unfair practices and claim there's some sort of big business collusion forcing out ranchers and farmers from their property in Tumble County. It's not my job to investigate it, but you and I both know where there's any hint of unfair practices and politics, the Judge is sure not to be far away."

"You do know that's your father you're talking about, right?"

"Yes. And it's more than likely the reason the lead investigator asked me to talk to him. To all outward appearances, I'm simply doing a routine check into their claims, but I'm hoping to do a whole lot more than that. I'm working behind the scenes with the Association to figure out what's going on before any other landowners end up on the chopping block."

"Great idea. Your dad would have a cow if he heard you were working with the Association, and it turns out he's on the other side. So how's the campaign going?"

Eric wasn't far off in his assessment of the judge. "Not as well as I expected. Harry said I'm falling behind because I'm not married and therefore not presenting the stable 'family man' image that most district attorneys have had in the past. He had the audacity to tell me to go round up a wife." The outlandish idea was still mind-boggling.

"Your career is everything to you. So do it. Jen has a friend she's been pushing me to introduce you to. Just make sure you're on the up and up with the woman or I'll never hear the end of it. Make it worth her while and you'll have no problem."

"You're kidding, right? When it comes to women and the word marriage, there are always problems. And you know I don't believe in it, anyway."

His friend might be okay with it, but saddling himself with a bride expecting a happily ever after, or at the very least half of his net worth, was like asking him to wrestle a crocodile. Chances were he'd lose.

"Don't condemn what you don't personally know," Eric said. "Marriage would be a means to get elected. Keep it in perspective. If you're to be believed, it's not like you're ever going to have a real marriage, so why not arrange a convenient one to your benefit? And hers, whatever it may be. You wouldn't be the first couple to do that, or the last. And who knows? Maybe if you spend enough time with someone, it might even work out."

"I think you spent too much time in Rome living and breathing love and it's addled your brain." Steve shook his head. A marriage of convenience? This was the twenty-first century, last time he checked.

Eric seemed to wave away the jab. "Whether you like it or not, Harry is probably right, and it's your best possible solution. If you change your mind, Jen's friend's name is Michelle. We can all meet for drinks or something."

"You're forgetting one thing. An arranged marriage takes two people. What would Jen's friend gain from a political match? Or would she be looking for a real relationship? Most people are."

"Just think about it. When are you getting back to Houston? Jen wants to have you over to dinner, which is why I was calling in the first place." Eric wasn't giving up, but Steve had no intention of giving in, either. Michelle could find her own man.

"Hopefully by Friday. I'm trying to get an audience with the Judge to get a sense of what's going on and the level of his involvement, and I've got a private meeting with the Association on Thursday."

"Okay. Let me know if there's anything I can do to help." They finished their call, and Steve hung up, Eric's words still ringing in his head.

Marriage.

Not if he could help it. He'd watched his parents muddle through their marriage with fights and anger until they finally got a divorce. It had been enough to convince him the state of holy matrimony was more like a state of hell.

Steve downed the rest of his coffee and headed out the door, his father's latest text vibrating in his pocket. Putting him off yet again—no surprise. Steve's thoughts drifted toward Becky and her situation. The woman needed help, but he wasn't sure she'd be keen on him being the one providing the help if what he suspected about Jack was true. There was only one way to find out the truth, and it started with asking Becky some point-blank questions. The fear in her eyes had been crystal clear, as well as her determination to leave once she had Jack's phone number. After he'd had time to think about it, his protective instinct had gone into operational mode, and there was no way he was leaving without answers.

He drove to Charlie's Diner, intent on talking to her, not only about her reaction, but also to learn more about Byron. And he wasn't leaving Riverbend until he had answers to both. Because the only thing he knew for sure was that his brother would never help Becky. Jack had only ever thought of himself his whole life, taking after their dad.

Steve parked his Navigator in front of Charlie's and made his way inside, the overhead bell ringing as he stepped through the door. "Welcome to Charlie's," the server at the bar called out and waved. "Have a seat and we'll be right with you." The table he'd sat at before was empty—a table he knew Becky would be serving—and so he made his way over to it.

Becky came through the swinging door, her gaze landing on him as she grabbed a couple of menus from the holder. She froze.

He smiled and waved, hoping to put her at ease after yesterday's awkward meeting. He hadn't helped by being a bit of a jerk, his shock at her being at the house and asking for Jack not settling well at the onset.

Becky spoke with the server behind the counter, the two women talking in hushed tones, Steve unable to catch their voices. The other server glanced his way and then back at Becky and shrugged. She took the menus from Becky and headed his way.

Interesting. It looked as though Becky intended to give him the cold shoulder.

"Welcome to Charlie's. My name is Katie, and I'll be your server. What can I get you to drink?" The young brunette smiled, none of Becky's coldness rubbing off on her.

"I'll have an iced tea," he said. "Is there a reason Becky doesn't want to wait on her own table?" Direct was the only approach he knew. Katie's smile faded right before she glanced down at her order pad and then over at Becky.

She turned her gaze back on him and shrugged. "I don't know. But I'm sure you know better than I do, since she's not wanting to wait on you. Maybe you should ask her that question yourself." Katie's smile returned, but this time not as bright. "I'll be right back with your tea. Today's special is creamy mac & cheese. I highly recommend it." She held out a menu.

"The special is fine. Can you tell Becky I'd like to talk to her? Tell her it's important. I just need five minutes of her time."

"Okay, but I'm not sure it's going to do any good." Katie shrugged.

Time for a different approach. "Can I ask you one other question?"

"I don't see why not."

"I noticed Becky has a son, Byron. Is she married to Byron's father?" He shouldn't have asked, and he knew it the minute the question slipped out. It was crossing personal lines.

"So that's what this is about. You're interested in her." Katie's brow notched upward, the question in her gaze unmistakable.

Steve wanted to correct her, but it was at least partly true. "Maybe." He grinned, hoping to gain a confidante in Katie.

"She's single. Never been married. And to the best of my knowledge, Byron's father's never been in the picture. You seem like a nice guy. Whatever you did to make her mad, you need to figure it out if you want a chance to take her out." She winked and walked away.

It was nothing more than he expected. The only line he wouldn't cross was asking for the name of Byron's father. He knew better than to ask anyone other than Becky for that information. He didn't claim to know much about women, but this much he did know.

"Becky," he called out as she came closer on her way to the kitchen. She slowed and looked toward him. "I need to talk to you. Please, it's important."

"I'm sorry. I don't have time to talk. I'm extremely busy." With only three other customers in the restaurant, she had to be lying, but he let it go. He wasn't going to bother her where she worked and get her into trouble.

Katie took good care of him for the rest of his lunch. He picked up his bill and headed for the register, where she met him to ring up the bill.

"What time does Becky get off work?" Steve asked.

"She's my friend, so you're putting me in a tough place. But I also know how stubborn she can be sometimes. She gets off at three. That's when she picks up Byron from school and takes him home." Katie handed him his change.

He smiled, dropping the few dollars and coins in the jar. "Thanks." He picked up the fundraiser jar, staring closely at the picture—more specifically, Byron's picture. There was some resemblance to the Parker family, though he still couldn't be sure. But it was the only thing that added up that would justify Becky's strange behavior. He hoped he was wrong, but he doubted it.

He jotted his number on the back of his receipt and handed it to Katie. "Here's my number. Can you give it to Becky, please? Tell her I have something important to discuss with her. And that if I don't hear from her, I'll be back tomorrow to sit in her section again, and every day until she talks to me. I'm not leaving town until that happens."

"You are persistent." Katie smiled.

You have no idea. "It's important," he repeated.

Steve left, intent on visiting a couple more local landowners, trying to get a sense of the impact the drought had on their farms and ranches. By five o'clock, he'd visited several, garnering bits and pieces of information that told of the dire straits several of them were facing. He also realized Becky wasn't going to call. It looked like he'd be eating lunch at Charlie's again tomorrow because he'd meant what he'd said—he wasn't giving up.

His phone rang, and Steve jumped to answer it, thinking—hoping—it was Becky. But Jerry Anderson's name lit up the screen. The president of the Cattlemen's Association must have something important to discuss because the meeting for tomorrow night had already been arranged. "Hey, Jerry."

"Hey. I heard you're in town already. Meeting's not till tomorrow night." The man was direct and to the point, a quality Steve admired.

"I know. I've been asked to check into some things by the lead investigator. Remember, though, I'll get more helpful information if nobody knows that I'm working with you."

"I understand. And I'm grateful you're trying to help. I know the position this put you in, but we need you." *Going up against my father?* Yeah, it was definitely a position, but Jerry was wrong thinking Steve didn't welcome it—he did. The chance to put his father in his place, more than worth it.

"So, what's going on?" Steve asked, curious what prompted the call.

"The rumors about the McDougall ranch are no longer rumors. Travis got his final eviction notice. He's got thirty days to make the payment to catch up his loan or they're seizing the property."

Unbelievable. "I wish there was something I could do, but four weeks just isn't much time."

"I get it. Just thought you should know." Jerry sounded frustrated, and rightfully so.

"Thanks for the heads up. I need to find out who's backing the savings and loan. There's got to be a connection we're missing." *Follow the money* was a good motto when it came to dirty dealings.

"Well, until we figure it out, this is just going to keep happening."

"I hear you." Steve ended the call and let out a deep sigh just as a text came through.

Harry: *Poll numbers just updated, and you slipped another two points.*

Steve cringed. His dream had been to advocate for those who needed a voice, and now his best shot at it was fading away.

Marriage. An arranged marriage. Jen's friend. Make it worth her while.

Becky's face came to mind. He needed to get married to have any shot at winning the D.A.'s seat, and she needed the insurance coverage for her son's surgery. Mutually beneficial.

A temporary wife.

"Temporary" had a beautiful ring to it, enough to be willing to put a ring on her finger and make sure they had an exit plan in place. It was the perfect solution. Becky was easy on the eyes and had a gentle spirit. How hard could it be to live with her and her son for a short time?

The more he thought about it, the better he liked the sound of it. But getting Becky to agree had one big problem—she wasn't even talking to him right now.

And the clock was ticking. He wouldn't be in town for long and waiting for Becky to come around and talk to him wasn't going to work. Left with no choice, he knew what he had to do. A couple of phone calls was all it took before he had her address.

At her place, they could talk privately. And with any luck, he'd get to meet Byron and see the boy who was possibly his nephew for himself. The very idea brought him an unusual and complex reaction. He was excited to think Byron could be the next generation of Parkers, something Steve never considered would happen, judging by Jack and his reticence to the holy state of matrimony.

But then came the fear the kid would turn out messed up like all the other Parkers and the very reason Steve didn't want children.

Chapter Five

♥

BECKY WAS OUTSIDE WATCHING Byron as he played on the sidewalk in front of the house. She sat on the porch stoop, laughing at his antics as he pretended to be a race car driver. It was by far his favorite game, and Becky worried he'd grow up and become a driver, something that scared the heck out of her. At times, she let herself dream he'd become a doctor, not that they could afford medical school. Luckily, those decisions were a long way off. She smiled at her son as he waved. Life wasn't fair, but they'd get through this like everything else.

A white Lincoln Navigator pulled up to the curve. Becky appreciated the caution the driver used having spotted Byron, the extra-slow speed obvious as the vehicle came to a stop.

"Byron, come here for a minute." She didn't know who it was, but people who drove such expensive vehicles didn't typically come around to this side of town and park. Becky had no qualms exercising her right to be overprotective.

"Coming." Byron ran toward her. "What is it, Mommy?" His sweet, innocent smile warmed her heart the same way it did every time he looked at her with his big, brown eyes.

"We have a visitor, honey, but I don't know who it is. You remember we had this talk about strangers and what to do?"

"Yes, I remember. I'll stay right here next to you."

"Good." Becky stood up, trying to make out the driver, but the tinted windows made it difficult. The door opened, and a man got out. As he came around the front of the vehicle, Becky recognized him immediately.

Steve. What was he doing here? And more importantly, how did he know where she lived? "Go sit on the porch, Byron. I'll handle this."

"Who is it, Mommy?"

"Someone I know from the diner. Do as I ask, please." She met Steve halfway down the sidewalk. "What are you doing here?" she asked, hands on her hips and not bothering to temper the tone of her voice. "How dare you come to my home."

"I'm sorry to show up unannounced, but I really do need to talk to you." He looked out of place, his dress slacks, blue dress shirt, and tie, not something often seen in this section of Riverbend. It did, however, surprise her that he didn't look at all uncomfortable.

"I don't owe you anything, and I'm not required to talk to you." She folded her arms in front of her chest as if to put a wall between them.

"However, you did agree to an ice cream date," he said, a teasing smile on his face. "One, I might add, you stood me up on. I'd say that entitles me to an explanation at the very least."

Becky frowned, although it didn't stop the tiny rush of pleasure that shot through her. Considering his displeasure when she'd arrived on his doorstep asking for his brother, the last thing she'd expected him to do was show up for their date. But it didn't change anything—Steve Parker was off- limits. "I broke the date. And?"

"Do you make a habit of going back on your word?" He took a step closer, his voice dropping a notch and becoming more tender. It made it harder to stay mad and harder to resist the kindness in his expression.

Becky edged back, finding it easier to stay focused if she kept her distance. She'd found him attractive and all too appealing before she knew who he was, and apparently her body and her brain weren't operating on the same wavelength. "I don't date, so no."

"That's nice to know. Makes me feel somewhat better." Steve stepped to the side and glanced toward the porch.

Becky reached for his arm, her heart racing as she realized his intentions. The last thing she wanted was for Byron and Steve to meet. "Byron, go inside the house," she said, using a gentle but firm voice, hoping she wouldn't scare her son.

"Okay, Mommy." Her son pulled the screen door open, prepared to do as he was told.

"Wait, Byron," Steve called out. "I was hoping to meet you, young man."

Byron paused, glancing back and forth between her and Steve, unsure what to do.

Steve was more observant than most people. Keeping Byron away from him was the best way to prevent Steve from connecting the very large dots she'd all but drawn for him. She sensed that if he had any inkling of the truth, he wouldn't let go. His tenacity might be a great character trait in the courtroom, but it wasn't anything she wanted used against her.

"Fine. Byron, this is Steve Parker. He's someone I met at Charlie's. He was a very generous donor toward helping with your medical expenses. Perhaps you should tell him thank you and then go inside and play with Julia there."

Steve extended his hand and shook Byron's.

"It's nice to meet you, Mr. Steve. And thanks for whatever a donor is." Byron smiled up at him.

"You're welcome, young man. But no thanks are needed. I just want to see you get healthy." Steve ruffled Byron's hair. Correction, *Uncle* Steve ruffled his hair.

Becky flinched, not wanting to acknowledge the truth, but unable to change the facts. "Now that you've met him, it's time for him to go inside. Whatever you need to say to me can be said out here. In private." The likes of a Parker had probably never stepped foot in a house like the one she lived in, and she wasn't about to let that happen today. Not on her watch.

"Yes, Mom. It was nice to meet you, sir."

"You too, kiddo." Steve smiled.

Becky let out a deep sigh of relief as Byron waved and headed inside, and Steve didn't try to stop him. She'd have to remember to tell Byron what an excellent job he'd done in both his manners and his listening to her later tonight when she tucked him into bed. Extra hugs and kisses were definitely in order.

She swallowed hard and turned to face Steve. "Okay, so now that you've met him, have you satisfied your curiosity?" Becky couldn't keep the edge out of her voice. This whole situation could blow up in her face, and after five years of staying off Jack's radar, she didn't want anything to change.

"Not really. Why did you stand me up yesterday?" Steve leaned against the porch post, his confidence far surpassing her own.

"As if that's not obvious. You're Jack's brother. That makes things a bit awkward." Especially given her attraction to the man. Something she hadn't felt for anyone in years.

"Awkward? You said you were friends. Can't you be friends with your friend's family?"

She hadn't realized how that sounded in the moment and wished she could take the words back. "No. That's not what I meant. It's just that...it made me uncomfortable. I really need to talk to Jack, and what I need to discuss with him is personal. I don't have time for new friendships, and I shouldn't have agreed to go to the ice cream parlor with you in the first place."

Backing out of the whole situation would be for the best, for everyone concerned. She had to put Byron above her own desires, ones that included Steve.

"Is Jack Byron's father?"

Becky jerked back, caught off guard by his direct question. "No! No, he's not." She corrected, trying to soften her automatic first response. The palms of her hand started to sweat as she twisted them, her rapid breaths causing her to feel lightheaded.

"Then who is?" His voice was soft and low, but the short and to the point question went straight to the heart of the matter and was the very information she'd kept to herself since the day she found out she was pregnant.

"That's none of your business." Hands on her hips, she faced him down, using a steely mask of reserve to cover the emotions threatening to take control.

"In a way, it is. I promise you, Becky, I only want to help." The man must be amazing in the courtroom given his ability to ask the right questions with unrelenting persistence.

Becky bit, her curiosity piqued just enough she couldn't resist asking the question. "How's that?"

"It's obvious Byron's father isn't in the picture. It's obvious you need help with medical expenses. And as an attorney who has made a dedicated effort to track down DBDs and make them pay, I want to make it my business to help you. I'm running for district attorney, and I plan to make it one of my primary office challenges."

"DBDs?"

"Deadbeat Dads." Steve stood there, nonchalant as he answered the question, but it was the tone in which he delivered the words that told her of his passion against dads who skirted their responsibilities.

Becky's admiration rose another notch. It was a personal passion of her own as well, just not one that she'd been able to do anything about. "Except you're not the district attorney."

"Not yet, but I'm counting on it." He shot her a grin that went straight to her heart. The man had a dream and a vision. Unfortunately, it didn't change anything for her.

"I haven't filed any charges or complaints, and although I appreciate your offer for help, I honestly don't need it." It was far too complicated and would never end well. For Byron and her.

"But I'm sure the question you were asking the other day in the diner wasn't for a friend. Am I right?" His gaze bore into her, as if trying to read her mind or her every reaction.

"I don't have to answer that. I think it's time for you to leave." Becky took a step toward the front door, reinforcing her request. The last thing she needed was for him to use his special courtroom skills on her and wear down her defenses. And she was pretty sure Steve Parker could do it, given the opportunity. There was something about him she wanted to trust, but it was the situation that wouldn't let her.

"Becky, wait. I have something else I'd like to talk to you about. Any chance we can go inside and speak like two normal adults?"

"A Parker in my house? That's a joke." She shook her head, the absurdity of it making her smile. "Whatever else needs to be said, you can say it out here." Becky wanted to hear what he had to say, not that it would make a difference. But she wouldn't give up the chance to garner useful information. No sense turning away free legal advice.

As long as she got him to leave before her mother came home, what could it hurt? Because one thing she wasn't prepared to do was explain why a Parker was planted on her porch.

"What's wrong with a Parker in your house?" The grooves of Steve's brow deepened as he looked back and forth between her and the house.

"You don't seriously need me to list them, do you? You live in a mansion with servants, ten bedrooms, six bathrooms, fine art, china, and a rolling expanse of land. I live here," she said, pointing to the house, "all two bedrooms, one bath, poster art, plastic dishes, and a tiny square of grass. Need I say more?" Becky scrunched her face up in disdain, the image in her head not an overly appealing one.

"There's nothing wrong with where you live. An old friend of mine lived in a place just like this when we were kids, and we played at his house by choice. Trust me, it's fine. It's the people inside a house that count."

Becky's mouth formed a wide *O*, a rush of unexpected admiration swirling through her. She'd known Steve wasn't at all like Jack. Well, except for the throwing money around part—she'd seen him in action at the diner. She'd think more about his answer later, but right now, she needed him to leave before her mother arrived. "Say what you came to say. I've got to get in and start dinner for Byron." She sat down on the top step, surprised when Steve sat down next to her, a move that set her heart to racing.

"Will you tell me what's wrong with Byron?"

Becky bristled, the question forcing her attention back to the reality of the situation. "No. That's private information. What's with the sudden interest in Byron? He's my son and no business of yours."

"I realize that, but I just want to help." The intensity of his gaze unsettled her because he looked as if he meant every word. "Did you ever reach Jack?"

"No. I tried, but the call went to voicemail. I'm waiting for him to call me back." It was more than she should have said, but Steve was easy to talk to. She'd have to be careful or he'd have her spilling her guts far more than she had with anyone else. And Jack's brother was the last person she should be doing that with.

"Good luck with that." Steve shook his head.

"What do you mean?"

"Jack's been gone for quite some time by choice. He's out doing what Jack does best—run the roads and party." Steve knew his brother well and clearly didn't approve. Her estimation of Steve rose several notches.

Becky let out a heavy sigh. Jack was her last resort to help Byron. She wasn't sure what she'd do if he wouldn't help. And until he said no, she had to believe there was a shred of decency in the man. "Let's just hope you're wrong."

"That doesn't happen often." His continued obvious derision surprised her. No love lost between the two brothers. The idea pleased her, even though it shouldn't matter.

"So exactly why are you here?" There was still the issue of her mother returning, and although she wasn't averse to talking to Steve, it wasn't a good idea. Not here. Not now.

"I have a proposition for you. I know it will sound crazy, but I promise you I've thought it through in great depth. I need your promise to hear me out...all the way. Will you promise me that much? In exchange for breaking our date." Steve grinned. His gaze never left her face as he waited for her answer. Her curiosity was in full swing, and there was no way she wouldn't hear out whatever idea he'd concocted.

"It wasn't an official date, and you know it. But yes, I promise to listen."

"I want you to marry me."

Nothing that could come out of Steve's mouth could've surprised her more.

"What?" she spluttered. "I don't understand why, but clearly, you're joking. What kind of a person jokes about something like that?"

"The kind who isn't joking. You promised to hear me out. Remember?" Steve took her hand as if to keep her from bolting, which was exactly what she wanted to do. The warmth of his hand settled her a bit.

She took a deep breath and exhaled. "There's nothing you could say that could make me believe you're serious about this."

"Here's the thing—it wouldn't be a real marriage. And it would only be a temporary one. An arranged, temporary marriage. One year max. Think of the benefit to Byron if you do this for me. You'll have the Parker name and insurance for Byron's surgery. Anything you need—for yourself and for him—it's yours."

"What's in it for you, then? What's the catch?" He was dangling a carrot in front of her face. A big, juicy carrot. Probably the biggest carrot she'd ever seen in her life.

"What I'm about to tell you, I prefer to remain a secret. I'm trusting you with the truth."

Becky nodded, unable to form a coherent answer.

"My poll rankings are slipping, and my campaign manager thinks it's because I'm not married and presenting family values to our constituents. I'm determined to win this election and willing to go to extreme lengths to make it happen."

Marrying someone for personal gain violated every belief she had, and nothing could induce her to marry a Parker.

Except Byron.

Another thought occurred to her, and it was a strong enough argument that almost made her say yes right there on the spot. Marriage to Steve would give Becky the added measure of protection she needed if Judge Parker and his ex-wife ever found out they had a grandson.

No. No way. It still isn't the right thing to do. "I can't. Byron is my problem, and I'll figure it out, especially since what you're suggesting could hurt and confuse him. I still have options, and they don't include marrying you. But out of curiosity, why the year?"

"I thought we should give ourselves a reasonable amount of time before splitting up. It would look better after the election and give you plenty of time to see to Byron's healthcare." Steve's honesty was refreshing, even if what he was proposing was absurd.

The irony of the situation hit her hard. A Parker had just asked her to marry him. Her first marriage proposal wasn't at all the way she'd planned when she used to do pretend weddings with Kayla as a child. "I'm sorry. I just don't think it's a good idea."

"I understand, though I'm disappointed. I really do have your best interests at heart." He stood, an air of discontent all around him.

Her heart went out to him, and she wished she could help, but circumstances being what they were, it wasn't possible. "Why is it so important for you to win?" she asked, trying to understand.

Steve looked away. It was the first time she'd seen him back down from a direct question. "I want to help people who need a fair voice in the judicial system. And yes, there's also a more personal reason, but I'd rather not share it, especially given that you've rejected my proposal. Suffice to say, the marriage would be good for both of us. I hope you'll reconsider." Apparently, they both had secrets they were unwilling to share.

"There's nothing to think about. The answer is no. I'm sorry."

"It really is a win-win. It's just two friends helping each other out." He stepped off the porch.

"Still a no. I'm sorry." Why did it bother her that she felt like she was letting him down?

Steve nodded. "Good night, Becky."

Long after Byron had gone to bed, Becky mentally replayed her conversation with Steve. A great guy had asked her to marry him. Her first proposal. It should have been special and filled with love, not a negotiation. *One year.* Then a divorce...

Byron would never understand, and she had to think of him.

The shrill ring of her phone broke the evening silence, and Becky dashed to pick it up, not wanting to wake anyone. The kids had gone to sleep, and her mother had to work early. She couldn't imagine who would be calling this time of night.

"Hello?" Becky spoke softly into the phone, the unfamiliar number not ringing any bells.

"You've got a lot of nerve calling me and asking for money." *Jack.* A voice she hadn't heard in a very long time, and judging by the slur in his words, not long enough. He always did have a penchant for whiskey. Some things never changed.

She tiptoed down the stairs and out the front door, not wanting to be overheard.

"I don't have anyone else to ask. You're his father. Please, Jack. You've got to help."

"I don't have to do anything. It's your fault you got pregnant. And the kid is your responsibility. Don't forget, your mother stills works for mine." His not-so-subtle reminder was exactly why she'd feared calling him in the first place.

"But he could die. Doesn't that mean anything to you?" She wasn't above pleading with the jerk if there was any way to convince him.

"I don't have time to play Daddy." His surly tone left her in no doubt it was a lost cause.

"I'm not asking you to. I've stayed out of your life and haven't asked you for a thing. But I need help. And you're the only one left I can turn to." *Except Steve...* She didn't want to think about that now.

"No. And if you breathe one word about me to anyone, watch out. You've already cost me my football career. I think I've paid plenty."

"How am I responsible for you not going pro?" His line of thinking was way off base, but then she shouldn't be surprised. Jack never took responsibility for his own actions.

"Women were the problem. And last I checked, you were one. Always distracting me, tempting me to party and have fun, skipping out on practices. You were all the same. Wanting more attention than I could give. At least you were the only one stupid enough to get pregnant. I can't imagine having other brats running around." His words made her flinch. Byron wasn't a brat. He was a sweet boy, the likes of which Jack didn't deserve.

Tears slid down Becky's face. As much as she wanted to holler, spit, and scream at the buffoon, she needed to hold her tongue. The last thing she wanted to do was cause him to make good on his threats. If her mother lost her job, they'd have nowhere to go. She had to think of the whole family, just like she'd always done.

"Never mind." She hung up before she said something she'd regret. All hope was gone. Becky brushed away her tears. All except the proposal Steve laid at her feet this evening.

One year.

Jack would be furious, but if she married Steve, it would end his ability to hurt her and her family. And Byron would get his surgery. Becky thought it over for a few minutes longer.

Marriage to Steve couldn't make things any worse than they were now, and it would solve most of her problems. *Blind justice.* Her son would have the Parker name, and they would ultimately be paying for Byron's healthcare, even if they didn't know his true identity. The biggest hurdle would be trying to keep Byron from getting hurt by her choices. Somehow, she'd make it work—for all of them. Byron's health was worth the risk.

It didn't hurt that her new husband also happened to be attractive. Her awareness level around him hadn't vanished, even knowing he was Jack's brother. Some things she had no control over.

She pulled the phone number from her jeans pocket and dialed before she chickened out.

Steve answered on the first ring. "Hello?"

"It's Becky. You have yourself a deal." She was going to do this. For Byron.

Steve's silence worried her. "Excellent," he finally said, the relief evident in his voice. "You won't regret it, I promise. Meet me at the entrance of Tucker's Park tomorrow night at six. We can go over the details." She could picture him smiling.

"That's a little public, don't you think?"

"Not at all. It's perfect for what we need. And, Becky?"

Her mind raced, trying to decide what he could possibly mean. "What?"

"Please don't stand me up this time. It's our first real date." She heard him chuckle just before the phone went dead.

Engaged. To a *Parker.*

For better or worse, she was getting married.

Chapter Six

♥

BECKY APPROACHED TUCKER'S PARK, Byron in hand. Her son would keep the outing a little less obvious and a whole lot less awkward. She spotted Steve, exactly where he said he'd be. He looked different. More approachable. Dressed in jeans and a cable-knit sweater, he looked good. Really good. So far, she'd only seen him in a standard suit, dress shirt, and tie, and she hadn't been sure until now he even owned a pair of jeans.

"Good afternoon, Becky. Byron, it's a nice surprise to see you again." Steve shook his hand, man-to-man, and her son stood just a little taller. Prouder. He didn't get much male influence in his life, and he was taking to Steve like a sponge in water.

"I thought it was a good chance for him to get some fresh air." Becky didn't quite look him in the eye, knowing that wasn't the whole truth. She was nervous, even if it was in part because of the man himself.

"Hi, Mr. Steve." He tugged on Becky's shirt. "Can I go play on the swing set? Big people talk is boring. And I see Johnny from school over there." So much for having her son as a buffer.

"I suppose that'll be okay. We'll be right over here if you need me." She pointed to the picnic table closest to the swings.

"Yes, ma'am." Byron ran off, all too happy to escape.

Steve, on the other hand, grinned as he watched Byron and then turned back to her. "I'm glad you brought him. I should have suggested it yesterday. I know what you were doing, but you forgot to take into account the playground drawcard." He chuckled even more, frustrating her.

"That wasn't my intention. I just thought it would be good for him to get out. My mom is still working, and Julia had lots of homework to do." Becky stood there with her arms folded across her chest, unwilling to confirm his view of the situation.

"Well, I think it was a great idea. Seals the deal even more, don't you think? If we're going to be one big happy family, the sooner everyone sees us all together, the better."

"I'm still not sure this is the right thing to do. I'm worried about the effect it will have on Byron in the long run. I worry about him becoming attached to you and getting hurt by all this."

She'd tossed and turned most of last night, plagued by this very thought. By the wee hours of the morning, she still didn't have any answers but was determined to make the best of the miracle solution that had landed on her lap.

Or, rather, on her ring finger.

"I'm concerned about it, too, but I can promise you, I'll do everything I can to make things right for him.

Even after we split." They walked to the picnic table and sat down next to each other.

"Thanks. I appreciate your understanding, and it makes me feel better to know you care. But exactly what do you mean?" Somehow, she had to reconcile this part in her head if she was going to make it work.

"I would never hurt him. He seems like a good kid, and I'm assuming we would part as friends and that I could continue to see him. He needs a father figure in his life. I'm not signing up for the role, but I'm sure it would do him good to see me on occasion. Maybe I could play ball or whatever it is dads do with sons. Although I may need guidance on that, seeing as my father only believed in working and didn't have time for kids." Steve's voice hardened as he spoke of his father, his facial lines deepening with tension.

Becky hadn't known her father, but she didn't harbor near the resentment Steve apparently did. "Seems to me you're following in your father's footsteps." It probably wasn't what he wanted to hear, but maybe he couldn't see the truth. The man lived and breathed law and his career. Just like his dad had done. Was still doing.

He looked at her, startled. "Why would you say that?"

"Just an observation. You're young to be a D.A., aren't you? You couldn't have gotten this far by being a slacker." Everything about Steve Parker reeked of success. His hair style didn't come from a barbershop. His clothes weren't from a department store. And his vehicle was top of the line.

"That's true, but I had a motivation, and motivation can be a great catalyst to achieving one's dreams."

"So what is your dream? Why is this so important to you?" She wanted to know more about Steve, and it wasn't all because of the marriage arrangement.

"To be the youngest elected D.A." He grinned and shrugged as if it was the most natural answer in the world.

"And why would you have that as a dream? That just doesn't seem like something a young boy would grow up saying. Like, oh, I want to be the youngest D.A."

Steve hesitated and let out a deep breath. "Seeing as you agreed to marry me, I guess it's safe to tell you. You are right about most boys not having the dream, but then most boys aren't the Judge's kid. I bet you didn't know my dad currently holds the record as the youngest elected D.A.?" He cocked one eyebrow up in question as he waited for her to answer.

They were getting somewhere, but what she heard was sad. "So this is about beating him?"

"Absolutely. But I'm not making the sacrifices he made to get there." He shook his head as if trying to gain her understanding.

"You mean by giving up his family?" she asked.

"Yes. I know what it's like to be on the receiving end of disappointment. The only thing important to that man is winning. And as his son, trust me, his standards were so high, no kid could meet his expectations. To his way of thinking, his sons would never amount to anything. Jack may have proved him right, but I was determined to be different—in every way. It's why I've chosen to never go down the marriage road."

And there it was—the full circle. Steve had laid all his cards on the table for her to see, but it didn't mean she agreed with his choices.

"Then technically, you're still making sacrifices," Becky replied. "You're preventing yourself from having a real life. So you're not different in that respect." She was good at giving advice but apparently not so good at applying it to her own life. Wasn't that the same thing she was doing?

"I suppose, but then you're making the same kind of sacrifices for your own reasons. How does that make us any different?" He was right, but it was unsettling that he'd put the two together the same way she had. It was one thing to put his life under a microscope, quite another hers.

"You're right. It doesn't."

Steve took her hand, his thumb caressing her palm as if trying to reassure her.

Except his touch was having the opposite effect. It was making her more nervous, her heart race, and her brain trip over itself as she tried to think of a way to shift the conversation back on track and away from where it was currently. "But here we are, getting married. Career aspirations just don't seem to resonate as a good reason to get married."

"That's true if it's a real marriage, but this is a marriage of convenience. No emotions. Temporary." Steve seemed so sure of everything, and she tried to feed off his confidence.

His opinion of marriage as a whole made her want to know more about him. "You have a very sour look on marriage. Why is that?" If they were going to get married, she needed to make it look convincing.

"Let's just say my parents weren't an exemplary example." That she believed, given his attitude and knowing Judge Parker and his wife.

"That's only one marriage. They're just two people in a sea of many. There are lots of other couples who managed to marry the right person." Even after all she'd been through, Becky still believed in happily ever after—she just wasn't sure it was in her cards.

"Not that I've noticed. But then I'm not looking. One of my best friends just got married, but they are still in the honeymoon phase and therefore not a reliable source of what the future will hold for them. But what about you? I don't see you running to get married—and you already have a son."

"That's just it. I have my son. I don't need anyone else—or I didn't until you came up with this ludicrous offer." She shook her head and laughed, still somewhat overwhelmed with the magnitude of what she'd agreed to.

"I thought most women wanted happily ever after?" His gaze never left her face, the scrutiny making her uncomfortable. Becky pulled her hand away and turned to watch Byron. She didn't like anyone looking too closely into what made her tick.

"Maybe when they start out as little girls reading fairy tales. But then real life happens, and they grow up. Some faster than others." And it's not that she didn't want it. The plain and simple truth was that true love hadn't come knocking at her door.

"That's a very cynical approach."

Better to let him believe she was cynical rather than a disappointed little girl who grew up but never let go of her fairy tale ending. "No different than your own." She shrugged, looking back at him.

"Well, okay, then. I've been thinking this through, and I believe it's important for us to move fast but to make it look real. It's a matter of finding the right balance, and that's what we need to discuss to land on the same page." Steve lowered his voice as a mother walked by pushing a baby stroller.

"I'm listening." Fast worked for her when it came to getting Byron healthcare coverage.

Steve grabbed her hand again, this time letting his fingers intertwine with her own. She tensed and started to pull away, but he tightened his grip. "You've agreed to marry me, and part of making this real is making the world believe we're a couple. Starting now. Try to relax. We're just two people enjoying the nice weather at the park with your son. Everyone needs to see us as a couple if they are going to believe we fell in love and decided to get married all of a sudden."

Becky relaxed, knowing he was right. The key was to remember what they were doing and why they were doing it. Otherwise, it would be all too easy to fall for his charm. And where would that leave her? She'd been down that road once before with his brother. The trick was guarding her heart so she didn't fall for any worn-out lines or extra attention he paid her. It was all for show. "So what is this grand plan you've devised?"

"I'm thinking we date for two weeks, get engaged for two weeks, and then get married. That brings us right up to the election, and in the frenzy of the media attention, I'm sure to gain votes. We can use the election as the catalyst expediting the wedding. It also gets the ball rolling to set up Byron's surgery. I looked into it, and you and Byron can be added to my coverage immediately with no concerns over existing conditions if I get married." He held her hand tight, his gaze locked with hers. She wasn't sure what she'd expected, but it wasn't this.

"Most people would use love as an excuse to get married that quickly. Either that or they're pregnant." Her history would set the gossips on fire with the possibility of a repeat, something she wasn't looking forward to dealing with, but for Byron's sake, she would.

"Good point. Guess everyone will realize it was love at first sight, then, because we know you won't turn up pregnant." He had the audacity to wink.

What concerned her more, however, was the slight thrill she got from his charming smile, the one he used on her when he teased. Surely, he wasn't teasing now. They hadn't exactly discussed that aspect of the relationship. "I'm glad you clarified that. No expectations. Right?"

"None. As far as I'm concerned, we need to make it look good, holding hands, kisses in public, the things normal couples do, but beyond that, we're two people doing the right thing and waiting until after we get married. And after the wedding, what happens behind closed doors, or separate bedrooms, is our own business." Steve managed to keep a straight face as he delivered the last comment but judging by the twitching at the corners of his mouth, it wasn't easy.

"I'm glad we agree on that part. But the kissing, do you think that's necessary? There will be nothing natural about it." Not to mention the fact she didn't want to fall for him, and who knew where kissing might lead? It was one thing to be attracted to him, quite another to act on the attraction and risk falling in love.

"I'm sure we can make it look good. I do think it's necessary, if we're going to sell this as the real deal." Steve leaned forward and kissed her cheek, catching her off guard. "See what I mean? The more I do that, the more natural it will look. Right now, you look like a blushing bride who's never been kissed."

"I can do it. You just took me by surprise."

"Good. Practice makes perfect, and I look forward to practicing with you." His teasing laugh curled her toes.

They walked hand in hand, following the sidewalk that looped around the play place. An awkward silence fell between them. For her, the kiss had muddled her brain.

"So now that you know my life story, what's yours?" Steve asked out of nowhere. "I'm sure that growing up, it wasn't your dream to be a single mother and a server at Charlie's?"

The conversation was suddenly right back where she didn't want it to be. The trick was figuring out what and how much to tell. "It wasn't. But I love Byron, and I wouldn't change a thing now." Becky was putting her trust in Steve in a way she hadn't done with anyone in years.

"So what was it? Let me guess, a nurse, or better still a doctor?" He grinned, the corners of his mouth crinkling.

Becky laughed. "No, the doctor thing I've got earmarked for Byron. Every mother's dream. For me, I just always wanted out of Riverbend. I used to dream of owning a coffee house in the city. A place where people came and talked every day, the hustle and bustle adding to the excitement." She shrugged but was unable to keep the excitement from her voice as she pictured her imaginary coffee shop. "I visited one when my mother had to take me to the city for something. I don't even remember what we went for, but the unique coffee shop with its nooks and tables and art deco called to me. Along with the fresh aroma of coffee grounds and brewing coffee." She laughed at her own silly memory.

Steve stopped walking and pulled her toward him. "What happened to make you give up the dream?"

Becky pulled away, casting a glance at Byron to make sure he was okay. "Life. Byron. Responsibility." She let out a sigh. "I wouldn't change it, though. I love my son more than anything."

"Are you going to tell me about Byron's father?" They were close—couple close—and it made her nervous. At some point, he would kiss her on more than her cheek, and she wanted to be prepared for the rush of emotions.

"No. It's complicated. Trust me, it's best left alone, for everyone concerned."

"Just so you know, I have my own suspicions, but I'll wait for you to tell me the truth. Can we at least talk about what's going on with Byron? Medically speaking."

"He's got an aggravated hernia and needs an operation. If left unattended, it can rupture and cause complications. In a child his age, it can be quite critical. The insurance deductible and copay were simply more than I could manage. I don't exactly have the kind of money for the best insurance, only the cheapest. And when something goes wrong like this, it takes a whole lot of cash. Cash I don't have." Having carried her burdens single-handedly for so long, she felt the comforting peace from sharing with someone else grow and grow until her heart felt lighter than it had in years.

Steve took her hand in his again, and she let him. "I'll take care of everything. You'll see. You don't have to worry anymore. I promise."

"Thank you." She meant it. It'd been a long time since someone had really taken care of her. It was a nice change. One that would be altogether too easy to get used to, and she'd have to keep reminding herself it wouldn't last forever. But for the next year, she'd find a way to make it work. And if Steve was taking care of everything, Becky would have the money from her job to continue helping her mother with the rent. Everything was working out perfectly.

Her only fear was the fury of Jack when he found out what she'd agreed to. With any luck, he'd stay out of town and never even find out about the wedding. But she wasn't holding out much hope for that to happen, considering he was family and sure to be invited.

They rounded up Byron and then stopped to pick up some Red Hot Chili dogs. Her son was in rare form, providing entertainment the whole time. It was a beautiful evening, perfect for a lover's stroll. Except they weren't lovers. Instead, they looked like one big happy family. Something else they weren't.

Steve walked them to her car when their strange date had come to an end. She managed to get Byron buckled into his car seat in the back without complaint, the poor kid completely exhausted.

Steve stepped in close, his gaze never leaving her face, the twinkle in his eyes a message she couldn't ignore.

"There are some people coming down the sidewalk. Perhaps this is a good time to practice."

She knew exactly what he meant. He was going to kiss her.

Part of her wanted him to, and part of her wanted to jump in the car and race home, especially knowing it was all for show. It was more than a little disappointing to know he was going to kiss her out of obligation and not because he wanted to.

He lowered his head toward hers, until they were mere inches apart. "Relax," he said, as if sensing her tension.

"That's hard to do. I haven't been kissed by anyone in ages. And you're going to kiss me because you have to. It's not very flattering." She hated the weakness in her voice and even more that she'd admitted the truth.

"That's where you're wrong. I'm going to kiss you because I want to. It's something I've wanted to do all night." He reached up to cup her cheek, his thumb sliding over her bottom lip.

She swallowed hard. "You have?"

"Yes."

"But what about the no-emotion rule?" It would be better if she just shut up and let him kiss her. Instead, the anticipation of the moment only intensified with each second she dragged it out.

"There's nothing saying we can't enjoy being with each other. If not, it'll be a long year."

He made perfect sense. Becky stopped resisting and closed the final distance between their mouths, because the truth was...she wanted it, too.

Steve's arms came around her, and he pulled her close, deepening the kiss.

She let her fingers sift through his thick curls, something she'd wanted to do for a while. The moment was like the stuff of fairy tales and dreams and happily ever afters.

Not real, but for now—perfect.

Chapter Seven

♥

STEVE STILL COULDN'T BELIEVE Becky had agreed to marry him. Sure, she needed the insurance coverage, but it had still come as a shock. It was real, and he would soon be engaged and married. Him. Steve Parker. The guy who swore to never get married.

But the bigger surprise was the time spent with Becky and Byron. Time he enjoyed, that he regretted when it had to end. Especially after their first kiss. It was true he'd wanted to, but he hadn't expected the rush of emotion he felt holding her in his arms. "Protective" and "caring" were the two best words he could find, any other description would be dangerous.

It was the first time in a long time he could remember talking to a woman about dreams and life in general. Someone he could relax enough around to actually have fun. Becky was easy to talk to and even easier to admire.

Raising her son single-handedly hadn't hurt her one iota, her zest for life encouraging after all the challenges she faced. She held down a job, juggled parenting, and all without remorse for the dreams she once believed in. The love for her son far surpassed any emotion in her voice when it came to letting go of her dreams. Her son was her dream, in a way.

Byron, it turned out, was a sweet and polite kid, which wasn't easy to accomplish in a society that craved instant gratification. Watching him play, Steve found himself captivated by the young boy's charm, laughter, and silliness. It was an age he didn't remember.

Steve had two parents, and neither one of them had given either him or his brother an ounce of the love Byron received every day. Not to mention the bonus of having her mother and her sister around to help. The child was surrounded by love...and it showed.

He glanced at his watch. Before word got out, he needed to let Harry know. His campaign manager would be thrilled, but if he wasn't given the heads up to capitalize on the information, he'd blow a gasket.

There was just enough time to text before tonight's meeting. It would also keep the questions to a limit.

Steve: *Met someone. She's amazing and sweet and has a five-year-old son. Truly unique woman. Wanted you to know before the media got wind of it.*

The arrangement between him and Becky was personal, and the details shouldn't matter. Harry should be ecstatic he was getting what he wanted, and he needed to protect Becky from everyone, even his campaign manager. It was a romance. End of story.

Harry: *Seriously? You took my advice? The election will be in the bag. It's just the twist we needed. Great job. I'll get someone to cover the budding romance right away. This is going to be great.*

Steve: *Nothing to do with your advice. Wonderful woman. Please make sure the media hounds go easy on her.*

Harry: *Now this is a surprise. Wonderful news. Leave everything to me.*

He trusted Harry would do his best with the media, but sometimes that wasn't always possible. Steve's protective streak had shifted into gear, and he'd make sure to keep an eye on things as well. The last thing he needed was for this to backfire and cause undue stress for Becky and her son. He'd do well to remember and warn her.

It was still a little early, but he planned to park a good distance away from where the Cattleman's Association meeting was taking place. People would be less likely to link his name to the group if they didn't suspect he was in attendance. The last thing he needed to do was have any of his dad's cronies notice him and report back to the Judge.

Steve drove down Main Street, scanning the area to make sure he didn't see anyone he knew, before parking the car. He chose a narrow back street to make his way to the meeting hall. The door was unlocked, and he slipped inside. The sound of raised voices drew his attention, and he headed in their direction. The men looked up as he entered the room, all voices ceasing.

"Good evening, Steve. Welcome. Come on in." Jerry stood and crossed the room to shake his hand.

"Most of you know Steve Parker, but for those of you who don't, he's Judge Parker's boy. He's come to find out more about what's going on with the Savings and Loan foreclosures and see what he can do to help. And he would appreciate it if his presence wasn't something discussed outside this room." Jerry clapped a hand on his shoulder, showing the men, as well as telling them, that he trusted Steve.

"Since when would Judge Parker allow anyone, especially his own son, to help us?" Except for at least one guy present, anyway. Not that he blamed the guy. He'd be a doubting Thomas, too.

"Now, now," Jerry said. "Settle down. You need to give him a chance. I trust him, which is why I reached out to him in the first place." Jerry was trying to control the situation, but the others joined in, voicing their doubts.

"Why? His daddy's authorizing every one of these foreclosures," another man huffed.

Steve wanted to take control before the meeting got out of hand. "Gentleman, that's why I'm here. Last time I checked, my name was Steve Parker, not Judge Parker, and I make my own decisions." He had heard the rumors of his dad's connection, although he wasn't sure they were rumors. And though his father was family, for Steve, the law came first. Something his father had taught him at an early age. Although, for Steve, the law meant upholding the rules established, not bending them for personal gain.

"Well, then, what do you propose we do to stop your daddy and all them other thieves stealing our land?" another man spoke up, this one in overalls and a grubby white T-shirt, looking like he'd just come from his fields.

"First of all, Judge Parker is the courtroom authority, not the bank authority. And it's the bank doing the foreclosing. Let's not forget that. Who's buying the land?

Anyone tracking that?" Steve stepped forward, closing the distance between him and the men. "I've already talked to a few of you, but I need as much information as you have if I'm going to help."

"Different people. City folk. And not one of them has done anything to do with the ten properties already foreclosed on in Tumble County. And I'm next on the chopping block." It was Travis McDougall, Sr. who spoke this time, the first property owner who'd approached him in Houston for advice.

"Not if I can help it," Steve assured him. "As a short-term measure, I want to set up an emergency fund for landowners. It's not free money, but a small loan to tide ranchers and farmers over and cover their payments until you all get back on your feet. It will serve to hold off any more foreclosures." He delivered the news, knowing it might be the final thing they needed to hear to give him a chance. To trust him. He might have left Riverbend, but it didn't mean the small town didn't hold a place in his heart. And these people needed hope.

"Where are you planning to come up with that kind of money?" Travis asked.

"I'm talking privately to some investors who might be willing to do short-term loans for a fee."

"Sounds like fancy talk for something that might or might not happen, and even if it did, it would be too late for me. I've only got thirty days. Nope, make that twenty-nine now." Travis's voice held a note of worn-out despair.

Steve nodded, letting out a deep breath. "I'm working on it, and Travis, you're first on the list of approvals."

"I don't want no charity. That land's been in the family for over one hundred years, and I don't want to be the one to fail, but charity, that just doesn't sit right in a man's craw." He knew Travis was a proud man. Most of these men were. And he needed to convince them it was a good plan.

"It's not charity. It's a short-term temporary loan, managed and overseen by someone we hire to monitor the situation. There are others who need help. Don't let pride get in your way."

"Well, it's not like I got a son to leave it to, anyway. So why fight it?" Travis huffed, his harsh words proof he still grieved for his son, even after two years. Steve had heard about the man going MIA in the army and then presumed dead. It had come as a shock to the community, one that rippled through the state of Texas and the country. Several others were lost in the same overseas assignment.

"Because it's your home. You still have your wife and daughter to think about. I hear your daughter is quite the horsewoman. Ever stop and think she might want the ranch?" Steve wanted to help, but McDougall needed to move forward in his thinking and past his grief.

"She's a woman. She should be getting married and having babies," he huffed. Several others nodded in agreement. Several of the older guys, he corrected. The younger guys shook their heads, not at all in agreement.

Steve laughed. "Quit living in the old world, Travis, and talk to your daughter. You might find out you have a lot to fight for."

"*Humph.* I'm not saying I will or I won't, but I'll think on it overnight." It was a start.

"As soon as I have the money, I'll set up the fund, but I want my name left out of this. No one can know who's putting all this together." Steve glanced around the room, making sure everyone here understood he meant every word.

"Afraid it will cost you the election? There's a lot of political power calling the shots nowadays, and with you running for office, you stand a lot to lose if they find out you're helping us."

The man had zeroed in on Steve's Achilles heel, but he wasn't about to enlighten him to the truth. That would require telling why, and so far, Becky was the only one who knew that truth about his relationship, or lack thereof, with Judge Parker. Even Eric hadn't heard the whole story. But Becky elicited his confidence, and he found her easy to talk to. "No. I just don't want credit. I only want to help."

The meeting lasted another two hours, every rancher taking the time to share where they stood and everyone trying to pitch in and figure out a plan of action. Dropping beef and produce prices in this region was just another example of the suspicious activity going on, the decrease making it even harder on the landowners to keep up with expenses.

By the time they'd finished, Steve had a pretty clear picture of the situation, even if it wasn't a good one. "Listen, guys, I've got to run. If you find out anything else, Jerry knows how to reach me. And Travis, you do your thinking while I work on the money." Steve was more than willing to make an early deposit with personal funds if necessary, something he hadn't bothered to mention to the proud group of men in the room. Casey

McDougall died serving his country, and Steve would do everything in his power to help his father save the McDougall ranch. It wasn't easy for Travis knowing his son would never return.

The attitude of the group toward him had shifted since his arrival, but there was a thin line between him and Judge Parker, and they all knew it. They were trusting him because Jerry trusted him, and now it was time to earn that trust.

Steve avoided his mother the following morning, not wanting to be subjected to any probing questions about what he was doing in town. The Judge had finally agreed to meet him this afternoon at Charlie's, which meant his time in Riverbend was drawing to a close.

He would have preferred somewhere else to have the conversation with the Judge, but his dad insisted he wanted to eat there. Steve was suspicious at his insistence, but it had taken him some time to force the meeting, so he wouldn't back out now. Besides, there was the added benefit of seeing Becky again, something he looked forward to a little more than he should.

And he knew—it was all in the kiss. Something in the region of his heart had stirred to life when her sweet lips connected with his. With any luck, he'd have a year of those kisses, and not just till the wedding.

He walked into Charlie's a few minutes late. His father was already seated toward the front, not in Becky's section. It was probably for the best if he was expected to concentrate.

The Judge glanced at his watch, knowing full well what time it was. "Nice to see you could make it."

Steve shrugged and sat, unwilling to rise to the bait but not against getting in his own shot. "Nice to see you could finally make it as well."

His dad's eyebrows shot upward, surprise written on his face. Then he grinned and nodded, conceding the hit. "Just busy. You know how it is."

"Yes, I do. It's always been that way for you."

"And you," he said, never taking his eyes off Steve.

"That's true." Steve hoped it was the only thing they had in common.

"Let's order first, and then we can talk about whatever is on your mind. Something warranted this lunch request." The Judge was still trying to maintain control, even when it came to lunch with his son. Some things never changed.

"The special okay with you? The board says it's macaroni and tomatoes on toast."

"How very uninteresting." Judge Parker's upper lip curled slightly at the corner.

"Everything I've eaten here has been great. I'm sure your twenty-dollar appetite will enjoy the five-dollar special." Steve grinned. "You were the one, after all, who insisted we eat here." Calling the Judge out as a snob felt good.

"Fine. Order away."

"Hey, Katie," he said when she approached their table. "Can you bring us a couple of the specials, please? And two iced teas?" he added.

"I'll take an IPA," the Judge corrected. "Need something to help wash down whatever it is we'll be eating."

"Make that two, then. Wouldn't want you to drink alone." Steve grinned.

"Or a case of still trying to be like your old man."

Steve rolled his eyes. "Doubt that. No one could be like you." It wasn't a compliment.

"That's true," the Judge admitted, cracking the barest hint of a smile. He gazed over at Becky and then back at Steve. "Word on the street is you were seen in a lip lock with our waitress."

"Your sources got it wrong." He wasn't even the least bit surprised his father had heard already. "It wasn't Katie. It was Becky. McAllister." It's not as if his father didn't know the truth. The old man was just testing him.

"I see. Trying to gain voter points for having a loving side to your image? Mingling with the townsfolk." His father might do business that way, but it had never been Steve's thing. Until now. The thought didn't sit well at all. The whole fake engagement and marriage were designed to gain him favor in the polls, his dad's comment striking far too close to home.

"Hardly." It was nothing he'd share with the old man. Sharing confidences was never part of their agenda.

"It worked for me. Although, in my case, I didn't have much choice. Be careful, son. Your Becky has already had one son out of wedlock. And you know that's how your mother got me up the aisle. It was a huge mess and almost ruined my career." Yes, how could he forget, since his father never missed an opportunity to remind him? Steve was an unplanned and unwanted baby.

"I know what I'm doing with Becky—don't worry." Short for *none of the Judge's business.*

Katie delivered their drinks and then moved off to help another customer.

His dad shrugged. "What is it you wanted to meet about?"

It wasn't over. Not by a long shot. But Steve knew his father would keep an eye on him and find out anything he wanted to know, no matter what resources he needed to use to get the information. "I just wanted to ask you about the McDougalls." His father's eyes narrowed, the lines of tension in his face deepening.

"What about them? Travis McDougall ran his ranch to the ground. Don't tell me he came whining to you for help? You need to stay out of it. He defaulted on his loan. End of story where you and I are concerned."

"But I thought things were getting better now that the drought is over. Isn't there any way to help him? That family has been in Riverbend since the beginning. They're a big part of this town."

"They let it get too far. Crying shame, but a contract's a contract. You know that as well as I do. It's not our job to get involved. Our job is to do what's right in the eyes of the law." The Judge sat back in the booth and took a long swig of beer, not at all concerned about the people.

"He lost his son not long ago. Doesn't the fact the man was a war hero count for anything to the bank? Or you? It's been tougher on him than most."

"I have to follow the law. He defaulted on his contract. I'm sorry, Steve, there's nothing I can do to stop it." Then why didn't he sound sorry? It all came down to the contracts.

Maybe it was time he read the loan documents Travis signed when he took out the equity loan to tide him through the drought.

"I'm sure you heard the Cattleman's Association has filed a complaint regarding all the recent foreclosures in the county. They've assigned an investigator to the case." Just a little prodding with public information never hurt. One little unintentional slip by the Judge could give Steve the boost he needed to figure out what was going on behind the scenes.

The Judge sat back, his hardened gaze focused on Steve. "I heard. Waste of time. Bunch of whiny guys looking to blame someone for their own shortfalls. You should steer clear of the investigation as best you can. Poking your nose in where it doesn't belong could ruin your chances in the election. Not that you're ready for the job yet, anyway." The Judge couldn't help but add the dig, his arrogance a familiar tune. But Steve also couldn't help but understand the warning in his words. He knew his father and his tactics all too well.

Steve chose to ignore the jab, staying focused on what was important. "I told the investigator I'd talk to you and see what you had to say."

"Nothing to tell. The drought hit them hard, and they're losing their ranches and farms as a result. End of story. You've wasted your time coming here and talking to the ranchers." Steve had wondered if he'd gotten word about the visits—now he had his answer.

"Seems that way." Steve nodded. He could be just as tight-lipped about things as the Judge.

"Heard your mother is having a surprise dinner for you tonight." The old man had lots of ears in town.

"Yes, she wants to show off her future-district-attorney son."

Steve wasn't oblivious to his mother's motives. It would have been nice if he could have spent the evening with Becky and Byron, but his mother had managed to put a kink in any plans he would have made. And unfortunately, it was too early to introduce Becky to his family. They'd find out soon enough he was dating her.

It's the rest that will blow them away.

"How's that going, anyway? Still trying to beat me out, are you? It'll never happen. You're too young, and the voters know it. Not nearly as experienced as I was at your age." His dad had the audacity to grin. "But it was a good try."

"We'll see about that." The election was still six weeks away, and hopefully, his family image was about to improve the ratings. At least, his campaign manager seemed to think it would. Steve sure hoped he was right.

"If you were experienced, you'd know this dinner party is because your mother heard about your new girlfriend, and she's hoping you'll bring her. You need to always look for the ulterior motive."

Truer words were never spoken. "Then she'll be disappointed. I'm not sure Becky's ready for Mother. We've only just met, and I've got a lot going on. It's not like I'm going to be swept off my feet and fall in love." The last part was the truth. Love was not on his agenda.

"That would be the kiss of death to your career. Mark my words. Do what you need to do with her and move on. Words of advice from your old man."

Words Steve could live without. "You've never been one for advice. Why start now?"

"I don't know. Old age?" The Judge laughed.

"I don't buy it. You want something from me. What is it?" Steve pressed for more information. His old man always had an ulterior motive if he was being nice.

"Just in case you do get the D.A. job, you and I would need to talk. We could do great things together. Profitable things."

His eyes narrowed. It was nice to know the Judge hadn't totally discounted the possibility he would win this election.

"Except there's one big difference between you and me, Pops." Steve leaned forward as if he was about to reveal a big secret.

"What's that?" One eyebrow shot upward, the Judge eyeing him closely.

"I'm not driven by money."

"Then what are you driven by?"

"Being better than you." Steve delivered the bomb he'd longed to say but had never voiced to the old man, an overwhelming sense of freedom washing over him.

The Judge laughed out loud, his shoulders shaking. "Good luck with that, boy." He nodded, tossing a twenty on the table, stood, and then turned to leave, making a grand exit. It was always his way.

But this thing between them wasn't over yet. Steve was positive his father was at least ankle-deep in the dirty dealings with the landowners, and he was determined to put an end to the foreclosures. He just hoped his father hadn't crossed any legal lines, because Steve intended to go after everyone involved. Even if it meant the downfall of Judge Parker.

Chapter Eight

♥

BECKY FOLDED BYRON'S PAJAMAS and put them in the drawer. "You need to finish getting dressed. Steve will be here any minute and we can go see Aunt Kayla."

"Yeah! I can't wait to see her and the horses. Can I really ride today?"

"Absolutely." Becky had been unreasonably disappointed when Steve called her yesterday and mentioned he already had dinner plans and couldn't meet up with them. And when he called last night to make plans for today, she couldn't keep the sudden rush of adrenaline that left her giddy with excitement.

He'd been totally on board with going to the Hunter ranch to go horseback riding. His enthusiasm was another surprise, but it was wonderful to know they had at least one thing in common. The next year of her life might be filled with rides, which wouldn't be so bad.

She smiled at Byron. "Kayla thinks you're ready for your first big-boy lesson and she's going to take you out of the paddock after you get warmed up—*if* you can show her how responsible you can be."

"Okay, Mommy. I can do it. I'll show you both. And Mr. Steve, too." His smile revealed a gap where the most recent tooth fairy acquisition had come from. Byron constantly talked about Steve, which was more proof he needed a male role model in his life. Perhaps God had answered her prayers in more than one way.

Her mother and sister only knew her new beau as "Steve." Not Steve *Parker*. When her mother learned the truth, she'd be more than a little suspicious, and Becky preferred it to be a case of a little too late when she found out. And it was only a matter of time before the rumor mill would carry his last name to her ears. And worse, judging by Steve's warning, that the media would find out that her mother's employer was Olivia Parker.

Somehow, she needed to find the right moment to tell them both the truth. It wasn't that she felt it would change anything, more that it would raise suspicions she didn't want raised.

Yesterday had been more than awkward when Judge Parker had walked into Charlie's, and not long after, Steve. At least he hadn't sat in her section. It was bad enough she found it difficult to keep her eyes off the pair, curious what they were meeting about, his father's glances in her direction more than once or twice a clear indication she was at least one of the subjects under discussion.

She'd edged close enough a few times to catch a little bit of the conversation, recognizing the name of Travis McDougall. The whole town knew he was being foreclosed on, and there were rumors of political connections and shady behind-the-scenes shenanigans

prompting the foreclosure. Everyone also knew the judge was highly connected with some of the deeper pockets. And based on the subject of their lunch discussion, it would seem Steve was also. What she didn't understand, though, was why? Especially because, by doing so, he was tying himself to the coattails of a man he'd professed to resent for most of his life.

Becky was having a hard time fitting together the two sides of Steve. The man was determined to win the election, but she wasn't sure it was for all the right reasons or that it was right to move forward with the engagement and marriage as a ruse. Getting in bed with Steve, literally, of course, was not something she would have agreed to under normal circumstances, but Byron's surgery wasn't normal, and she was desperate.

Sometimes, though, Steve managed to break out of office mode, as she now liked to think of it, and have fun. Byron had that effect on people, her son refusing to fade into the background when he wanted attention. And male attention was the highlight of his life at the age of five.

Becky's focus had to remain on Byron, and Steve's activities were of no concern to her, but if she learned of anything that would help the Cattleman's Association fight back against the crooks, she'd share. Her allegiance would be to the town, not her temporary husband. And certainly not a Parker.

"Brush your teeth and hair and come downstairs. I want to pack us a picnic lunch."

"I love picnics! This is going to be a great day."

She smiled at her son's enthusiasm.

Becky packed the basket and grabbed one of the spare blankets from the closet, picking one that wasn't faded from hundreds of washings. She put everything by the front door, anxious to be ready to leave and keep Steve from having any reason to come inside. Despite what he said about his childhood friend, she was embarrassed to have him see where she lived.

She watched out the window, grateful when Byron came down the stairs just as Steve pulled up to the curb. As he strode toward the house, her breath caught, the sight of him causing a flush of pleasure to course through her. It might all be fake, but there was nothing fake about her attraction to him. Something she'd do well to make sure he didn't find out. And something that would be difficult to do if he continued kissing her.

"Let's go, honey. He's here," Becky said as she picked up the basket and headed outside, meeting Steve at the steps.

"It's great that you're eager to see me, but I didn't expect to rush off. Don't you want to introduce me to your mom? I'd love to meet her." Steve didn't move, emphasizing his words.

"*Umm*, she's at work." Becky shrugged. "Maybe next time. I didn't want to keep you waiting since you were gracious enough to want to go with us today."

"What? And miss the chance to get back on a horse? Never." Steve kneeled next to Byron. "Hey, kiddo, you ready to go riding? I heard you've got a big day today."

"I sure do. Aunty Kayla's going to let me ride out of the paddock with her." Byron's eyes were lit with excitement.

"Auntie Kayla? I thought Julia was your only sister." He looked up at her, his brow wrinkled in confusion, and stood.

"She is. Kayla's my best friend. Byron likes to call her Aunt."

"I see. It's nice you have a friend who's like family. I'm sure it's good for Byron."

Becky wasn't about to get drawn into a conversation that involved Byron's family or lack thereof. It was a rocky subject with the brother of Byron's father. Too many times she'd questioned her choice about not letting the Parkers know about their grandson, but in the end, it had been too risky to chance. Jack had made the decision for her, but still, she wished Byron could have had a bigger, loving family.

"How long has it been since you were on a horse?" No matter how long, she was liking the way he looked in jeans and the cotton flannel shirt tucked in. No sign of the city-slicker attorney. Becky preferred this Steve Parker the best.

"Since I was about fourteen. Too long, the way I see it. I used to love riding." He loaded the picnic basket and Byron's car seat in the back of the Navigator.

"Why did you quit?"

Steve paused, a sheltered look falling across his face as he glanced toward the backseat where Byron had climbed in, waiting to be buckled in. "Let's just say my motivation and choices changed for the worse." She could tell he didn't want to say more. At least not in front of Byron. She'd have to ask him about it later.

Several vehicles pulled up behind Steve's SUV, and suddenly, the place was teeming with reporters and cameras, flashbulbs popping off repeatedly. Fear ripped down her spine, her throat constricting. Steve's warnings didn't come close to the reality of having someone stalk them for photos. And information. Becky closed the door to protect Byron from the fray and then watched as Steve moved to talk to the group.

"Hey, everyone. I realize you're here for a story, but Becky and I are just friends. Not overly newsworthy."

"Not according to Harry," one of the guys called out. "He smells love in the air."

"Harry's a romantic at heart. If you leave us alone, I promise I'll call you if anything changes and there's a real story for you to cover." Steve knew his part well and was obviously used to dealing with the media. Becky, on the other hand, was a bundle of nerves and couldn't wait to escape, hoping they wouldn't follow them. Kayla wouldn't appreciate the reporters on her property any more than Becky liked them here invading her personal space.

"Fine. Just remember you promised," one of the women spoke up. The cameras flashed a few more times, and then, true to their word, they left.

"Sorry about that. I was wondering how long it would take them to show up. That should buy us at least twenty- four hours." Steve grinned.

His attitude didn't even come close to the way she felt. "I don't know how you deal with it all the time."

"You get used to it. I'm sorry. I promise to do my best to keep it under control."

Probably not. They got in the car and drove off, Becky relieved not to see anyone following them.

Byron talked nonstop on the short drive to Kayla's, telling Steve all about Sugar, his favorite horse. Which was good because it gave Becky time to prepare what she was going to tell Kayla and Dylan about her future wedding plans and why she was doing it. Not being upfront and honest with her best friend six years ago had cost them their friendship for some time. They'd only recently repaired the relationship, and now she was afraid she'd lose it again. Enough so, she knew there was no choice but to tell her friend the truth.

Kayla might not like her decision to marry Steve and would try and talk her out of it. But then Kayla was completely in love and recently married and wanted the same for Becky. Once Kayla realized Becky wasn't going to change her mind, she'd support the decision. And right now, she needed someone in her court.

Steve turned down the driveway that led to the Hunter ranch, the dry dirt road leaving a cloud of dust behind them. *Got to love the dry Texas air this time of year.* Kayla came out of the house as they pulled up. It didn't take Byron long to spot her, and he unbuckled his seat belt and bolted out the door.

"Hey, honey." Kayla picked him up and swung him around, just as excited to see him as he was her. Becky smiled, the sight of them together always bringing tears of joy to her eyes.

"Thanks for doing this, Kayla." Becky hugged her friend.

"No worries. I love hanging with this little guy. We're going to have so much fun today." Kayla set him down and looked up at Steve with interest. Her friend was protective of her and hadn't been able to disguise her interest in learning more about the man Becky was bringing riding. Something Becky hadn't done before.

"Great. I'd like you to meet Steve Parker. Steve, this is Kayla Hunter." He stepped forward and shook hands, completely at ease meeting new people.

"Welcome to the ranch. Becky's told me all about you, and I'm glad you were able to join us. It'll be nice for Byron to have you both along to show off his new skills. Helps build confidence." Kayla smiled and shook hands with him.

"Thanks for the invite. I'm a little rusty at this, so I hope you have a gentle horse for me." Another point for Steve. Honesty. Which was completely at odds with her assessment of him yesterday in his dealing with his father. Question was, who was the real Steve?

"You'll be fine. Riding a horse is like riding a bike—you just need to get back on." Kayla laughed.

"For my body's sake, let's just hope you're right." Steve shook his head and joined in the laughter. He didn't seem to care he might be the object of the humor.

"Dylan got caught up in town, but he's hoping to meet us later. I've got the horses saddled and ready to go if you all are."

"I'm ready, Aunty Kayla!" Byron took off running toward the barn.

"I brought a picnic lunch. I thought maybe we could strap it on one of the horses and eat down by the river," Becky offered.

"Great idea. Let's go."

Steve retrieved the picnic basket, and they made their way to the barn. Byron was there, carefully stroking the side of a horse's neck and mane, talking to the white mare. It was a one-sided conversation, but for a boy of five, he didn't seem to mind.

Steve lifted Byron into his saddle and handed him the reins. They looked like father and son, the image almost too much to take in. Aside from their wavy brown hair and firm jawline, it was the unusual shade of dark brown chocolatey eyes that were almost black and long lashes that stood out. The question was, did Kayla notice the resemblance? Or was it only because she knew just how close to family the pair of them were?

Kayla hoisted herself into the saddle. "If you two want to ride around the area a little while I walk Byron through the basics as a reminder, it'll be like ten minutes or so."

"We'll stick around and watch, if that's okay with you, Becky. Byron can show me how it's done." He winked.

"Yup. I sure can." Byron beamed, excited to teach a grown-up something.

"Let's start really slow and walk around a little to see if you remember the rules," Kayla suggested.

"Yes, Aunty Kayla." The two of them moved around the outer perimeter of the paddock.

"He's pretty good. All joking aside, he might show me up out there." Becky enjoyed Steve's sense of humility and his humor. It was the total opposite of his brother, a guy who thought the world was his for the taking and didn't care who he stepped on along the way. How could two brothers be so different?

"You'll be fine. It was a sweet thing to say, and I'm sure it did his confidence a world of good. He gets plenty of the female version of praise, and it might be more meaningful coming from a man."

"I'll remember that. When I was a kid, a little praise now and then would have gone a long way. Shall we saddle up?" Every time she got a glimpse into Steve's past, the man closed down by changing the subject. A year was a long time to not get to know someone.

They saddled up, Steve looking like he'd done it a time or two. Maybe a little stiff, but the guy hadn't forgotten the basics. They pulled up next to Kayla and Byron, the horses dancing a little with nervous energy, ready to be off.

"Look, Mom. Look, Mr. Steve. I'm doing it!" Byron's happy smile was firmly in place as he walked the horse around the pen all by himself.

"Yes, you're doing great," Becky encouraged him.

"I was just telling your mother you were going to show me up out there. You're a much better rider than I am." Steve nodded, equally showing his appreciation of Byron's skills.

Her son beamed under the compliment. "Don't worry, Mr. Steve, I'll show you how if you forgot. Just watch." Byron urged his horse forward, swinging around to see if everyone was following him.

"Go ahead, Byron. We can head down the trail through the pasture for a bit." Kayla rode next to Byron, keeping a close watch on him.

Becky and Steve followed, letting the others set the pace. She loved riding the trails at the Hunter ranch but unfortunately didn't get too many opportunities. On one side, the pasture with its long grass swept the countryside as far as the eye could see, bordered by woods. The other side, of course, fenced in the special herd of cattle Kayla and Dylan raised.

Steve glanced around. "This is a nice piece of land. I'm sure it's been in the family a long time. It looks like you could ride into the sunset."

"Yes, Dylan put everything he had into the place after his father died. He also managed to save Kayla's family farm. Then they got married and now it's all one huge property. Those cattle over there," she pointed at the herd, "are all organically fed cattle. Turns out there's a huge market for the beef, and Dylan has done well. If he hadn't been able to save the farm, the place would have gone by the wayside and been sold off to whoever's been buying up property around here. Shame no one can stop these people."

She hadn't meant to venture down this road but now was as good a time as any. Maybe she'd finally find out which side he'd land on, although she was very much afraid it would be on the side of family. Parker family.

"I've heard about it. What do you know?" The intensity of his voice increased, alerting her that he was very interested in the topic. He was definitely involved.

"Not much. Mostly rumors." She knew she wouldn't tell him anything specific at this point. "You heard about the McDougalls since you've been in town? They lost their son, Casey, in the war not long ago. Things have been tough, and now the bank is pushing them off their land." This was supposed to be a relaxing ride, but the subject matter was anything but.

"I've heard. Doesn't sound like much can be done, though." Or nothing a Parker would do to help. The judge could step in if he wanted to, force the bank to give them more time.

"No, not unless you've got large amounts of money you want to part with," she teased, trying to lighten the conversation.

Steve frowned, his brow drawn tight as if she'd hit a nerve. "Seems to me you know more than you're saying."

She should have shut up when she'd had the chance. It wasn't a good subject, and based on the stiff set of his shoulders, he agreed. "Sorry, I was only teasing. Relax."

"Good. I talked to the insurance office and the administrator at Houston General and got everything lined up for Byron's surgery. All we need is a wedding and the money." He changed the subject faster than the tornado winds that occasionally blew through the valley.

Becky was torn between relief and guilt. "How did you manage that? I can't believe they would even discuss it with you. And when exactly is our wedding?"

"It's one of the best hospitals in Texas, and I know some people who knew some people, and they pulled a few strings to start the process."

Oh. Wow. "Thank you," she said. Glancing up at Kayla and Byron as they rode ahead, she couldn't help feeling a sense of pride as she watched her son ride. He was sitting up straight and eagerly taking in Kayla's instructions as she tried to show him how to handle the reins and steer the horse. Becky slowed her mare, patting the side of her neck, feeling the glistening sweat from the ride. "I really was just teasing earlier. As to the date, the sooner the better, I reckon. For Byron's sake. Just tell me when to be at the courthouse." She needed to remember this was just a business transaction.

"I'm a private person when it comes to finances, and trust me, most people don't understand what drives me, and I don't like to be judged. I had enough of that growing up." Becky wasn't sure why he said what he did by way of explanation, but it was a start, and she had no intention of steering clear of the subject if he was in share mode.

"Your father doesn't sound like a very nice man." She glanced at him, trying to gauge his reaction.

"He's not." Steve grimaced, as though thinking of the past pained him.

The horses had fallen into a steady pace, walking side by side, an occasional snort as though they too were having a conversation. "I thought you two were getting along pretty well yesterday at the diner."

"It was business." Unlike most people, Steve didn't have to like his father to do business with him. Exactly what she'd been afraid of.

Another crisp and final answer designed to close the subject. Seemed there were a few subjects they had to tiptoe around. "How did your plans work out last night? You didn't actually say what you were doing." She'd been more than a little curious but afraid to be too inquisitive.

"My mother had a dinner party to show off her son. It was boring and nothing you would have enjoyed. People are talking in town about us already, and I think she was hoping to meet you. I thought I'd give you a little more time to get adjusted before that happened." He grinned.

Good call. "Thank you. I would have been way too nervous." Even if she had the entire year to prepare, she would still be nervous. But then she had good reason for not wanting to get too close to Steve's parents.

They'd fallen behind Kayla and Byron, enough for Becky to ask the question that had been weighing heavy on her mind. "While they're out of earshot, I need to ask you something. This marriage deal we are planning on, how do you propose it's going to work after we're married? I mean, I'm sure you're not planning on staying in Riverbend. And then there's your election coming up soon. When are you heading back to Houston?"

Steve shrugged. "I thought I'd stick around for a couple more days and then head home. I was hoping you and Byron would visit on weekends. We can announce the engagement soon and start planning the wedding. The distance can be the catalyst to get married sooner. Then we can get Byron transferred to a Houston school close to my apartment. You can get a job there if you want, or not. The choice is up to you."

Transfer to Houston. It was the first she heard about this part of the deal. "I don't recall agreeing to move anywhere."

"You don't sound like you're happy with the plan." Steve's gaze sharpened, his brow drawing tight in confusion.

"I'm not. It would have been nice if we'd talked it out because then you would have found out I'm not willing to leave Riverbend. I'm not pulling my son out of school and away from his friends for some fake marriage. And I'm not going to live off you like a parasite for a year, and I'm not giving up my job. It's not just me your plan affects, it's Byron, my mother, and my sister."

"I didn't think you wouldn't want to move with me to Houston. You said you always wanted to live in the city.

I thought you'd jump at the opportunity. It would seem I was wrong about you." He frowned.

"If you win the election, you're tied to Houston, but I'm tied to Riverbend either way. This is my home. And you're right, once upon a time, I dreamed of leaving, but the town has been loving and supportive toward Byron and me, and I've come to realize this is where I belong. A town where people know your name and help one another. People who truly care." She sighed, shaking her head. "I'm not sure this is going to work."

"We'll figure something out." He shrugged again as if the details were insignificant. "Even if it's a week-end-only marriage, we'll make it work. We have to."

It might be for the best, anyway. Spending quality time with Steve was easy but not something she wanted to get so used to. It would only make it harder for her and Byron to give it all up when the marriage ended.

Chapter Nine

♥

STEVE HAD TOLD HARRY about Becky, but he hadn't bothered to let the man know what was really happening, preferring to keep the arrangement more private. The fewer people who knew the truth, the better. For his campaign manager, it was all about the poll numbers, and it was not surprising he'd been the one to leak the information to the media.

Harry kept pushing him to stay in Riverbend, but Steve had to keep up with his job at the same time. Spending the weekends with her and Byron would be enough to make the relationship look real when he suddenly popped the question.

It was all about image, and the Riverbend festival tonight was the perfect opportunity to promote the image of them as a couple. Not that they hadn't had plenty of curious gawkers at church this morning. It had been the first time he'd been inside a church that he could remember. Something else his parents had never done. But for Becky, he'd agreed when she asked. The surprise, however, had been the calmness and peace he felt as he listened to the sermon on forgiveness, which had touched his heart in ways he hadn't expected.

But tonight was a different matter entirely. He wanted to spend time with Becky and Byron, dancing and laughing, the draw for a different taste of life beguiling. His world was all law and business meetings and courtrooms. Somber. Serious. Boring. *No fun.*

It would be cooler after sunset, the night air dropping as much as ten to fifteen degrees in temperature. He pulled a tan sweater over his blue dress shirt and stepped back to check out his new outfit in the mirror. New boots and a cable-knit sweater to wear with his jeans would be a whole lot less businesslike. He was grateful to be able to find what he needed with little effort at the Farm Supply shop in town and wasn't forced to drive back to the city. Satisfied with the look and appreciative of the comfort, he turned to leave. On second thought, the boots might take a little longer to call comfort, the stiffness of the leather not giving much as he walked, but they'd have to do.

He drove to Becky's place, anxious to see her again. Pulling up to the curb, he slid out of the car, determined to meet her at the front door and make it a proper date. It was time to meet her mother. The door opened as he drew near, and the two of them came outside, just like before.

Becky didn't understand that he didn't care what the house looked like, only the people inside. As she stepped off the porch, Steve stopped to appreciate the picture they presented. Mother and son. Becky wore a pretty blue-and- white gingham dress that stopped above her knees and showed off her gorgeous legs. The blue of her cardigan highlighted her eyes and the twinkle of excitement he'd noticed. Her hair was in a bun, but blonde curls interlaced with blue ribbons framed her face, softening the look. He hoped her look of excitement was because they were going on another date and that at least some of her emotion was genuine.

Byron, on the other hand, was dressed much the same as Steve was, except with a navy-blue sweater. He looked handsome standing next to his mother, his hair perfectly groomed, the same eager look in his eyes.

"Good evening. Nice night for a dance." He leaned forward and pulled Becky in for a brief hug, dropping a light kiss on her cheek. He felt her stiffen. They both knew they needed to progress the dating look to anyone watching, and he was relieved when she hadn't stopped him. But her resistance stung more than a little.

"It is, isn't it? Byron's been so excited." Becky pulled back, wrapping her arms around her midsection.

"Hey, Mr. Steve, we're dressed alike."

"That was the first thing I noticed." Steve shot Becky a wink. They both knew Byron hadn't come first in his appraisal. "Guess I did right picking out my new duds."

"You're kidding! You had to buy new clothes for the festival?" Becky smiled and shook her head.

"The sweater and boots, yes." He laughed. "Not much call for sweaters at the office."

"What's with the blue shirts, anyway? It's the only color you ever wear."

"Blue goes with all my ties. Simplifies everything." He wasn't about to get into the idea the power image he was trying to create as a professional dictated his choices, or that the deep-seated reason he wanted everything organized and orderly in his life stemmed from his father's dictatorial parenting style.

"If you say so." She leaned in toward him. "But when we get married, I expect something different once in a while, like a white one. To spruce things up a bit if you know what I mean." She smirked. "Make it special."

He took the car seat from Becky. "Whatever makes the old lady happy." Steve flashed her a grin and was rewarded with a playful hit to his shoulder. At the truck, he opened the passenger door and let Becky install the seat before he helped Byron up inside. Becky climbed in, careful to keep the skirt of her dress from riding up, but not before Steve got a little extra glimpse of leg and a whiff of sweet jasmine. Tonight, he'd be the envy of many a single man at the dance with Becky by his side.

"Look, Mom, look." He leaned forward to grab Becky by her sweater and tugged. The kid had spotted the Ferris wheel and merry-go-round rides and pointed to them.

"I see. Looks like big fun." She looked back at her son, love in her gaze.

Steve shook his head and smiled. The pure, unadulterated joy of a child was catchy, and he found himself watching the boy in the rearview mirror, loving the wide variety of expressions that crossed his face as they parked.

Becky held Byron's hand, but the kid tried to pull away, wanting to run ahead in an effort to expedite his way to the fun. "Come on, guys."

"There's plenty of time. I think we should eat first, kiddo. What do you say?" Becky looked at Steve for confirmation, but Byron had his own opinion on the subject matter.

"*Nawww.* Play first, please," he begged.

Becky shrugged. "Okay, three fun things and then we eat. Deal?"

"Deal." Byron was all too ready to agree. Compromise wasn't something Steve remembered when he was a kid. With the Judge, it was always his way or the highway. Or it was until his father took the highway himself.

"Where to first, Byron?" If Steve was doing the picking, he knew which one he would have picked first. The Ferris wheel.

Byron thought about it long and hard, suddenly smiling. "The Ferris wheel."

"And why is that?" Steve doubted it was the same reasons he had as a child. Curiosity made him ask.

"I like to go high and dream of flying. Someday, I want to be a pilot and fly everywhere."

"Big dreams, kiddo. I like it. Maybe one day you'll fly me where I want to go. That would be cool." Byron's reason wasn't too far off from his own but was way more uplifting.

"You really think I could?" Byron stopped to look up at him, his eyes wide with the question.

"Of course, you can. You can do anything you want to if you work at it hard enough." Just like he'd done and was still doing. His focus had been to help those less fortunate, and after years of hard work, it was about to pay off.

"Do you hear that, Mom? Mr. Steve said I could be a pilot."

"Yes, honey, and I agree. Let's head for the Ferris wheel and let you pretend you're already soaring high above the clouds. All three of us can fit, and maybe you could tell us what you see up there."

"Yes!" Byron ran ahead to mark their place in line.

"You don't mind, do you?" Becky asked.

"Not at all. Ferris wheels were my favorite when I was a kid. I can't wait to see if that's changed." He smiled, more than a little caught up in Byron's excitement and the idea of spending time going on the ride, with Becky closely tucked in by his side.

"Why was it your favorite?" Becky placed her hand on his arm, increasing the closeness between them.

He found himself wanting to share more with her. "It was the one ride that took me high enough to see far, far away. I always dreamed of leaving Riverbend."

"Sounds like we had that in common. But life doesn't always go as planned. I'm glad you got to leave, and your dream is in sight. It must be an amazing feeling."

"Surprisingly, it's been somewhat anti-climactic so far. I fully expect the high to hit me soon, or maybe it will happen after the election. Did you stay because of Byron?"

Becky stiffened beside him, her answer slow in coming. It was clearly a sore subject for her, but he wanted to understand what happened, especially given the circumstances and his deep suspicion of who Byron's father was.

"I got pregnant, and his father wanted no part of raising a family. I did what I needed to do to keep my son, and that meant giving up silly dreams and becoming a responsible, working parent. I don't regret anything I gave up. Byron is my life, and I'd do anything for him." Her voice radiated with warmth as she spoke of Byron.

"I can see that. He's a lucky boy to have you as his mother."

"Thank you. That's a very sweet compliment."

He glanced up to where Byron stood in line waiting for them, waving his arm as he gestured for them to hurry up.

Steve took Becky by the arm to get her to stop for a moment, not wanting Byron or anyone else to hear his next question. Becky couldn't evade his answer forever if he had anything to do about it.

She looked up at him, her brow furrowed. "What is it?"

"I know when we first talked, you didn't want to tell me about Byron's father. I have a strong suspicion it's Jack and would love for you to confirm or deny it."

"It doesn't matter who he is. Byron's father made his choice, and I'm okay with it." A shuttered look came over her face.

"But what about the father's family? Don't they have the right to know? The right to decide if they want to help you financially or not?" His family. Him. They had a right to know Byron, whether Jack wanted them to or not.

Becky stiffened, the line of his questioning clearly pushing her too hard. "No. It's...it's not Jack, so you don't need to worry about it. Jack and I were friends. End of discussion." Either she was lying, or he'd been wrong. His gut told him the former. But questioning her any more now would only make things worse.

"Okay. I'm sorry. I only want to help. I hope you can see that. Don't forget, I'll soon be your husband." He winked, hoping to put a smile back on her face.

"Don't remind me."

Ouch. The only saving grace to her comment was the slight curling of her lips as she fought back a smile. Steve hadn't missed her slip of the tongue. *Were friends.* Not *are* friends, as in currently friends, but past tense. Even more reason to suspect Jack was the father. And if it was Jack, she stood to gain financially and socially, so why lie? If she was lying, she was giving up the birthright of her son, not to mention, his nephew. The legal side of his brain wanted answers, but the social side said to let it go and have fun with her and her son. At least for the moment.

During the ride, Byron painted them a fairy-tale picture of his version of flying, his story filled with imagination. Steve could almost see the birds flying with the plane and the angels on the wings carrying the plane and its passengers to safety. Byron was such a sweet boy, one he would be proud to call family. It was shocking to realize he, the man who put career above all else, meant every word. But then, being a fantastic uncle would be like being a grandparent. Mostly pros and few cons. Grandparents were there to have fun with until they needed to get back to business and return the child to their parents. Or parent, in this case.

"So, what did you think? Is it still your favorite?" Becky glanced up at him, her sweet smile melting a region of his heart immune to emotion. Her eyelashes fluttered as she blinked, waiting on his answer.

"It was good. Not the same, mind you. Suddenly, things aren't so far away." He joked, knowing she'd understand. Growing up had a way of changing someone's perspective. It was the first time he could remember being on a Ferris wheel that he wasn't planning his escape out of Riverbend. Instead, thanks to Byron, he'd flown around the country in a magical world. Personally, he liked Byron's version better.

They did a couple more rides as promised before Becky announced it was time to eat, and surprisingly, Byron didn't argue. The kid must have worked up an appetite.

After standing in line and placing their orders, Becky found them a picnic table, and he waited for the food. He carried back a tray piled high with some of the festival favorites—chili, BBQ ribs, corn on the cob, fried green tomatoes, and fried okra. One of his personal favorites.

There was enough food to feed them and several others, the portions overwhelming. Not like what he saw in upscale nouvelle cuisine restaurants in Houston. He shook his head, getting full just looking at all the food. But not enough to say no to the delicious aromas wafting his way.

"Oh my, that looks amazing." Becky smiled and reached to help remove the food from the tray, placing it all in the middle, family-style. She laid out the paper plates and plastic utensils while he passed out loads of napkins to each of them.

"Can I have a rib and some corn, please?" Byron asked. "I love corn."

"If you're not careful, you're going to turn into a piece of corn." Becky laughed and ruffled his hair. She picked up his plate and placed a rib and half an ear of corn on it, adding a helping of okra. "Do you want some chili?"

"No thanks. You know what they say, beans, beans, they're good for your heart, the more you eat—"

"That's enough, young man. A simple yes or no will do." Becky fought back a grin.

"No, thanks. But it's true. And I don't want to fart." Byron had the good graces to look perfectly innocent as he said the word.

Becky couldn't hold back the grin any more than she could stop from bursting out with laughter. "You're hopeless," she added, shaking her head.

Steve chuckled, unable to see the problem. Farting was a big part of a boy's life and saying the word even bigger, especially if it embarrassed your parents. At least it had been until the act of having fun had been curtailed. Becky didn't seem to be afflicted with the same snobbish problem his own parents had. Lucky Byron.

"Sorry, Steve. He doesn't understand it's not polite."

"He's fine, trust me. Right, kiddo?" Steve bumped shoulders with the boy.

"Yup. See, Mom? Mr. Steve's cool with it." The kid grinned like he had a new best friend.

"Thanks." Becky shook her head. "When he first started repeating the rhyme, I listened to it over and over before I finally put an end to it."

"Sorry. Hey, Byron, how about we make a deal? You say the rhyme when only I'm around and no girls. It hurts a lady's sensibilities." He grinned.

"What's senbililities?"

"Sensibilities are their delicate nature of what's proper and not." Steve bust out laughing, unable to hold back any longer. Being around Byron and Becky, he found himself laughing quite a bit. He didn't even mind the photographer he'd noticed keeping an eye on them from a distance. A few photos wouldn't hurt but could certainly help his poll ratings if Harry was right. They finished their meal and cleaned up the table just as the sound of music drifted their way. The band was warming up, and it wouldn't be long before the sunset and the stars of Texas lit the sky for a romantic and fun evening of dancing. Steve might have been to the festival before as a kid, but the dancing part was something he'd never experienced here. And tonight, he was more than looking forward to it.

On the way toward the dance floor specially laid out for the evening, Steve had a sudden urge to do something silly—like win his girl a teddy bear. On a whim, he grabbed her hand and pulled her toward the basketball hoop shooting game.

"What are you doing?"

"You'll see." They stopped at the basketball hoops.

"Byron's got a lot of stuffed animals already. You don't have to do this." Becky shook her head at him, but she was smiling.

"But who said it was for Byron?"

"Give it a try, mister?" the operator called out.

Steve laid down a twenty-dollar bill. "Keep them coming until I win"—he glanced at the prizes—"that one." He pointed at a big floppy-eared brown bear with a red heart on his chest.

"You got it, Mister." Steve took his first shot and missed.

Becky giggled, but at least Byron cheered him on.

The next few shots were just as bad. Steve pulled out another twenty and slapped it down on the counter.

"All or none on one?" he asked, feeling good about the next shot.

"Steve, stop. You don't have to do this. You're going overboard in trying to make it look like a good idea." She spoke softly so no one else could hear. But he heard, and she was wrong.

"This has nothing to do with that and everything to do with you." He grinned and dropped a kiss on the tip of her nose.

She blushed prettily under the fluorescent lights, and Steve was pleased to be the one to put a little color on her cheeks.

"If you say so." She shook her head and stepped back to watch him waste another twenty bucks, but he intended to make this shot count.

"Watch closely." He grinned.

Becky giggled. "You know, you could buy it at the store for less money."

"I know, but it wouldn't be the same. You won't cherish it as much as you will if I win it for you. Am I right, buddy?" He glanced at Byron, looking for man-to-man agreement.

"Yup. I still remember all the animals I got from the fair. You should see the one Mommy won for me once. I love it lots, 'cause we don't have the extra money to play games all the time, but she did it once for me for my birthday."

"Well, there you have it," Steve agreed.

Becky's face and throat turned splotchy with various shades of pink. Byron, on the other hand, didn't have a clue what he just revealed. Steve decided it was best to let it go, but it was all the more reason to talk to her about Jack again sometime in the future. But tonight, it was all about fun.

Steve lined up his shot, taking several practice air shots to get a feel for the arc he needed as if the past ten weren't enough. With one last look and a smile at Becky, he turned back and shot the ball. Time seemed to slow as he watched it go up and hit the rim, bouncing in the air and then falling in the net. *Yes.* He pumped his fist in the air like a little kid.

"You did it! You did it! Mommy, he won."

Over Byron's head, Steve glanced at Becky. Her eyes were filled with tears, and she brushed at them with the back of her hand to clear her vision.

The operator handed him the prized teddy bear, a smile on his face. "Nice job. Gutsy, but it paid off. People do the wildest things for love."

"Yes, they do, don't they?" He grinned and turned to Becky, holding out her teddy bear.

"I can't believe you did it. You're such a kid at heart, you know."

"That's 'cause I care about you." He handed her the bear. This whole thing was supposed to be an act, but now, he wasn't so sure. He'd have to be careful or he'd do the unthinkable and actually fall for her. For real.

Becky threw her arms around his neck to hug him and whispered in his ear, "The least I can do is thank you properly considering all the effort you're going to show the folks around here that we're an item."

Maybe it was already too late. Her words weren't exactly what he wanted to hear. He would have preferred the exuberant thank-you to be genuine. Steve was seeing a side of life he'd never experienced before. Family life. *Happy* family life, to be exact. And he liked it. It was more fun than he'd had in a long time. And while the thought should be unsettling, at the same time, it wasn't. "You could dance with me."

"I could." She smiled.

They walked over to find a table near the dance floor. "Byron, can you sit here and keep an eye on the teddy bear? I want to dance with your mom."

"You like her, don't you?" Byron asked, his smile more than enough to realize the kid might already be imagining something more permanent.

"I do." He winked. Speaking the truth out loud felt amazing, even if he couldn't affirm that truth to Becky. It wouldn't do to let her know how much he'd enjoyed holding her or the desire he'd experienced not to let her go.

Steve led her onto the dance floor and pulled her close, relishing the feel of her back in his arms. The curious stares of others surrounded them as they danced to "Stars Over Texas," a fitting song to kick off the night. Becky let her head drop against his shoulder, her sweet jasmine scent teasing his senses.

"You shouldn't encourage him. Are you sure we're doing the right thing? I worry about him."

"Absolutely. I'll make sure no one gets hurt."

"You keep saying that, but you can't guarantee it."

"Maybe not, but I can promise I'll try." They were two different people with different goals and life plans. The only thing they were on the same page about was the temporary solution to their immediate problems. Anything other than that would be foolish and could jeopardize everything he'd worked for all these years.

Chapter Ten

♥

BECKY FILLED THE SALT and pepper shakers, topped off the catsup bottles, and filled all the napkin holders on each table. It was the quiet after-lunch lull. With only one customer to wait on, it gave her plenty of time to think.

Or too much time, depending how she looked at it. Ever since the dance, people looked at her funny, as if wanting to ask about her and Steve's relationship status but having the good graces to refrain. Luckily, the photo in the tabloids of Steve and a woman locked in an embrace hadn't identified her, the huge teddy bear blocking out her face. It wouldn't be long before the dots were connected, forcing her to face the truth. It was time to tell Steve. No more putting it off.

At first, she'd been terrified of Jack getting wind of the situation and making trouble for her. Steve had unwittingly counseled her on Jack's parental rights, and it gave her a small measure of reassurance, but she still didn't want trouble. The deal with Steve solved her money problems, and Byron would get his surgery, but

Becky felt guilty not telling Steve the truth about what he was stepping into.

Once Jack heard, it was bound to blow up in her face, but with any luck, he'd stay gone until it was too late. Pitting brother against brother would never end well—for her or them.

Her cell phone vibrated in her pocket. She pulled it out to check the message.

Steve: *How's your day going? I should be in town shortly after five. I know this is last minute, but my mother wants to meet you. She planned another one of her spur-of-the-moment dinners for tonight. Six. Please say yes. I think it's time we move to the next stage of our plans.*

Becky: *Why?*

Steve: *Why does she want to meet you? Because we're dating.*

Becky: *Who will be there?*

Steve: *Just her and the Judge that I know of.*

Becky let out a sigh of relief. She knew this time would come, and it was good to know there was a silver lining in the meeting. Jack was still out of town.

Becky: *Okay. I'll get my mother or sister to watch Byron.*

Steve: *Perfect. Don't worry, I'll take care of everything. We're doing the right thing. Pick you up at five-thirty.*

His reassurance didn't do anything for the guilt and fear warring within her. She agreed to this plan, and for Byron's sake, she'd see it through and face the devil himself if she had to. Even if the devil had Jack's face.

She got off work at three, and by the time she got Byron from school and home, she wouldn't have much time to get ready. The idea of formally meeting his parents was daunting. Knowing he planned to announce their engagement soon pushed her closer to freaking out. There was no way the influential Parker family would approve their son marrying someone of questionable background, especially given her mother was in their employ.

When Steve arrived to pick her up for dinner, Becky was determined to finally introduce Steve to her mother. Once the engagement was announced, it would be too late, and the last thing she wanted was for the people she cared about to find out from the media—and they *would* find out. The favored candidate for district attorney getting engaged would be big news.

A cold, gooey sensation against her fingers made her look down. *Ugh.* Catsup overflowed from the bottle and over her hand, making a huge mess. That's what she got for thinking instead of paying attention to what she was doing.

The next hour raced by, her dread increasing by the minute. Before she knew it, she was back at the house and faced with the challenge of what to wear. Nothing she had would fit in with the sophisticated polish of the Parkers' expectations. After settling on a long beige cotton skirt and white long-sleeve blouse, she found a sweater to match, completing the ensemble.

She stepped back to look in the mirror. *Frumpy.*

Welcome to my world, Steve Parker.

Julia looked up as she came down the stairs. "Going out with your boyfriend again?" She grinned.

"*Haha.* What do you know about it?" *Hopefully nothing.*

"I heard from one of the kids at school he kissed you." Julia plopped down on the sofa.

"Thought you were supposed to be learning at school, not gossiping."

"It's not gossip if it's true. And we do have a thing called lunch. And homeroom. And after school."

"I saw him kiss her," Byron chimed in. "I like him. We have fun. When are we going to do something fun again, Mom?"

"I'm meeting him for dinner tonight, but I'm sure you'll see him tomorrow."

"Does that mean he's your boyfriend? Do you love him? Is he from around here?" Julia sat up, suddenly very interested.

No time like the present to spill the news or at least pave the way for it. She wouldn't breathe a word until Steve made it official. "Yes, he's my boyfriend. Yes, he's from around here, but he lives in Houston now. And love, it's too early to tell. Maybe. I don't know." She shrugged.

"Wow, really? Does Mom know?" Julia moved to the edge of the bed, eager for more information.

"Not yet. I didn't want to say anything until I knew if this would go beyond a few dates. Speaking of Mom, where is she? I was going to have her watch Byron for me." Becky glanced at her watch.

"I'll do it until she gets here. She said something about stopping by the grocery store on her way home. I don't mind helping so you can go out with your dreamy man. I've seen him through the window. Good-looking for an older guy."

Becky hadn't counted on her mother being gone. "He's not old. But yes, he's very handsome." The man would be downright swoon worthy if she was into a guy like that. Which she wasn't. She didn't have time for dating. Which was why the idea of getting married, even for pretend, threw her for a loop.

"You never date, so I'm happy you met someone nice. If you got married, would you move to Houston?" Her sister frowned as if suddenly remembering that tidbit of information.

"It's a little early to be talking about marriage and moving." *Hours early, but still early.* "He should be here soon. Thanks for watching Byron. I was hoping Mom would get to meet him when he picked me up, but maybe you could let her know I want to introduce him when I come home. Don't let her go to bed early tonight." Becky laughed. After dinner would have to suffice.

"You know she's anxious to meet him. She's been asking me all sorts of questions, none that I could answer. You've kept this guy under wraps."

Knock. Knock. Saved by the arrival of said guy.

"He's here!" Byron jumped off the bed, raced down the stairs, and pulled the door open just as Becky hit the top landing.

"Hey there, little buddy. How you doing?" Steve ruffled Byron's hair as he knelt to his level. Then he straightened and stepped inside the house.

"I'm good," Byron said. "What kind of fun are we going to do tomorrow?"

"I'm not sure yet. We need to make plans with your mom." Steve glanced up at her and then around the room, his appraising glance taking in everything, his expression giving away nothing.

An attorney never gives away his inner thoughts.

"Hi, there. Right on time, I see." He was dressed in his normal suit and tie, like tonight was a business meeting. In a way, she guessed it was. Something she'd do well to remember.

"I am. You look lovely." Becky blushed, his words contradicting her business meeting philosophy.

"Thank you. You look handsome. Like always."

"So you're a sucker for a suit and tie, then? Nice to know." He winked.

Julia had crossed the room to stand next to her.

"Steve, this is my sister, Julia. Julia's going to keep an eye on Byron till my mother gets home."

Julia shook hands with Steve, a perplexed look on her face. "It's nice to meet you. Finally."

"Likewise." Steve grinned, turning to Becky. "I was hoping to meet your mother." He leaned forward and dropped a kiss on her cheek.

"She's not here, sorry. But I've told Julia to make her stay up tonight to meet you when we get home."

Julia and Byron watched with avid interest.

"Progress. Thanks. I didn't want to think you were keeping me a secret." He winked at Julia, his grin widening.

"Why would I do that?" Becky swallowed hard, his words a little too close to the truth.

"You tell me." Steve eyed her, curiosity written across his face.

"We've got to go. In bed by eight-thirty, mister." She kissed Byron good night and gave him a hug.

"Good night," Steve said. "Get a good rest so we can have fun tomorrow. I've been looking forward to this weekend all week." He ruffled Byron's hair affectionately.

"You hear that, Mom? He's looking forward to seeing us," Byron crooned.

"I heard." Becky couldn't help but smile. It might be all for show, but her son was eating up the attention.

Steve walked her to the truck and opened the passenger door. She slid inside, letting him close the door, and then came around front to slide in next to her.

"I'm sorry I don't have anything fancier to wear. I know your mom is way more fashionable," Becky muttered.

"I'm not interested in what my mom wears. I meant what I said—you look lovely. I like fresh country appeal. Trust me." The man made her feel special even when he didn't have to, and Becky found herself liking it, much to her consternation.

"You do?"

"I do." His gaze held hers for longer than necessary as if he wanted to say more. She waited, wanting him to say more. Steve brushed her hair back from her face, his touch gentle.

Her heart beat faster.

"I'm glad you agreed to tonight." He leaned forward and kissed her.

Becky responded to the warmth of his mouth, urging him to continue. She shouldn't, but then again, why not? They were getting married, and kissing Steve was no hardship. The past five years, she'd had a sum total of zero kisses from an admirer, but Steve's kiss made it worth the wait. The guy sure knew how to make a woman feel cherished.

Steve pulled back and chucked her chin. "We're a team tonight. I'll take care of you, I promise." He started the car and pulled away from the curb.

"I believe you." Right now, she'd believe anything he said. The car was filled with his presence, and his strength empowered her to face his parents. It was the first time she would have entered his home as a guest, maybe also the last. She hadn't been there since she was seventeen, back when Jack first made a pass at her, making her believe he cared.

She shoved aside memories of him, not wanting to let them ruin her evening.

Steve told her about his week as they drove to his parents' house. She loved hearing some of the stories, the craziness of people's logic mind-boggling at times. He was trying to put her at ease, but the minute they pulled into the driveway, any ease she'd felt vanished.

The butler came out to wait on the landing for their arrival. Her last run-in with the man hadn't gone so well.

"Good evening, sir. Your mother and father are in the tearoom and waiting for you."

"Thank you, Randall. This is Becky McAllister, and she'll be dining with us this evening."

Randall cast her an appraising glance, one eyebrow rising higher as he recognized her. "It's nice to meet you, ma'am. Again." He stepped aside to let them pass.

Panic filled her as they stepped into the foyer. She reached out to grab Steve's arm to stop him. "Steve, wait. Before we go in there, there's something I need to tell you."

Steve looked at her, his eyes full of curiosity. "Now? Okay. We can step into the library for privacy."

They only managed two steps before a woman called out, her voice demanding. "Steve? Where are you going? I told Randall we were in the tearoom. We've been waiting for you."

"Yes, Mother. I thought I had time to show Becky around the house."

She was grateful Steve had a ready excuse, but unfortunately, telling him about her mother's employment would have to wait until later tonight. After dinner and when they were away from the mansion. A time when no one would see his reaction, for he was sure to be upset when he learned the truth. Too many people would have a field day with the rich son and the housekeeper's daughter as an item.

"Come along, dear. Your father has already arrived. You can do the introductions all at once." Her crisp tones were enough for Becky to know this wasn't a happy meeting. Mrs. Parker wasn't thrilled her son had a girlfriend. The woman's reaction was bound to be ugly when she learned the truth.

Becky stayed tucked close to Steve's side as they followed his mother into the tearoom. The room was decorated with fine art, Persian carpets, fancy duvets, lounge chairs, and a side bar, all of which wouldn't even fit in her living room. And this was just the tearoom.

No wonder her mother was tired every night she came home.

She knew that coming here, there was always the chance Mrs. Parker would recognize her, but she hoped the social queen had taken very little notice of the hired help's family.

Even if said employee had worked there for well over twenty years. And it's not like Jack ever brought her home to meet the parents.

"I'm surprised my father showed up. He's normally good for making plans and then blowing people off. But then, I've never brought a woman home, so this is big news to them."

"Never?" No wonder Mrs. Parker was in formidable queen mode.

"Never. I told you, I don't do relationships." Words to live by. Words she'd do well to remember. But it was hard when the man kissed her, making her forget reality.

Steve took her by the hand and led her to the tearoom. "Relax," he whispered as he pushed open the door and walked in.

His father watched as they crossed the room, rising to greet them. Tall and stoic, Judge Parker held himself aloof as if he were presiding over a courtroom and not in his ex- wife's tearoom.

"I'd like you to meet Becky McAllister. Becky, my parents, Olivia and Thomas, otherwise known as Judge Parker." Steve held one hand, giving her strength to get through the ordeal.

"It's nice to meet you both." Becky offered her hand in greeting. She'd been fortunate to not have ever met the judge in or out of the courtroom, but she had been around Steve's mother a couple of times when she was younger and had visited her own mother at work.

"Pleasure." Olivia Parker's faint handshake was delicate and sophisticated, just like the woman. Dressed in a dark blue skirt suit, white blouse, and overstated jewelry that reeked of wealth, she had her perfectly coiffed hair piled high on her head. But it was the cold assessment as she looked Becky up and down that left Becky reeling with worry.

Becky turned to Judge Parker and shook his hand. The man's large hand engulfed hers, his overbearing confidence shining through and making her more nervous. This man wielded a lot of power in the county and wasn't one to be crossed lightly.

"You must be special. Steve doesn't usually date or bring women to his mother's home. I'm surprised he's got time, considering the election." The older man shook his head, clearly unimpressed by his son's decision to date or his choice of companion.

Becky desperately searched for the right words to say, her nerves making her almost tongue-tied. "He does stay busy, but we manage to spend whatever time we can together."

"Oh, I hadn't realized things were that serious," his mother said, returning to her seat.

"Get the girl a drink, Steve." His dad spoke, crossing the room to the bar, expecting Steve to follow.

Steve looked at her for confirmation. She appreciated the gesture and nodded, knowing she'd have to get used to holding her own around these people. They were rich and sophisticated, not untouchable.

Becky sat down on the couch closest to his mother.

"How long have you two been an item?" His mother wasn't above prying.

They hadn't really discussed what they would say, so she stuck with the truth. "A couple of weeks. We met when he came into Charlie's."

"Charlie's? As in the bar?" she asked, distaste evident in her voice.

"It's also a restaurant. I'm a server there."

"I see." The condemnation in her tone indicated she might see but didn't like. Becky hadn't expected a warm welcome, but she hadn't been prepared for bold rudeness.

"He's a busy man and has a bright future ahead of him. I'd hate to see someone get in the way of that if you know what I mean." Becky hadn't been here even five minutes and the gloves had come off. But if anything, her words rallied Becky's flailing spirits.

"I know exactly what you mean, but I think what's between us is private. I will tell you this, though. I would never hurt your son or do anything to derail his career. We both have his best interests at heart." Becky wasn't sure where the bravado had come from, but it felt good standing up to the woman. Granted, it wasn't much, but it was a start.

Steve returned and handed her a glass of white wine. It was nice he'd remembered her telling him once what she liked. Poor guy looked tense and uncomfortable, but there was no way to ask him about it.

The conversation turned to Steve's campaign and his run for the D.A.'s office. His father seemed to think he was pushing too hard and that voter confidence levels wouldn't stand behind a young guy compared to the qualifications of his running opponent who had at least seven more years of experience.

His mother, on the other hand, thought her son highly accomplished and ready, pushing her ex-husband's buttons by bringing up the fact Steve would surpass him as youngest D.A. elected if he were to win.

Back and forth, the conversation heated up, barely concealed distaste evident. The good part about it, though, was they didn't look to include her in their disagreement, leaving her to sit quietly and mind her own business. Steve tried to include her at times, but she knew better than to offer any real opinions on the subject.

His mother glanced at her watch. "Dinner should be served soon. I can't imagine why the others aren't here yet."

"Others?" Becky asked, suddenly alert.

"Yes, my other son and his cousin were supposed to be here. I called him this morning and mandated his presence for such an auspicious family occasion as his brother bringing home a girlfriend."

Her other son. *Jack.*

Becky could feel the color drain from her face, a sick feeling landing in the pit of her stomach. She closed her eyes, fighting back the wave of nausea that threatened.

Steve took her hand and gave it a squeeze, trying to reassure her. She should have told him the truth.

"I see. If you'll point me to the nearest bathroom, I'd like to excuse myself for a minute." Becky was in a panic and needed time to regroup. *Maybe run.* She would if she had a vehicle.

Steve stood at the same time she did and placed his arm at the small of her back.

"I'll show her the way." He led her across the room.

The door opened, and Jack walked in. His gaze landed on Becky and instantly turned to one of shock and then disgust. "Steve." He nodded.

"Jack. Sorry Mother dragged you away from your playtime to come to dinner." Just as she suspected, there was no love lost between the two men.

"What Mother wants, Mother gets." He smirked, his hard gaze never leaving Becky. Waves of nausea threatened to overwhelm her.

"That's true for you, anyway. She's still controlling your purse strings." Steve took a direct shot at his brother's failings.

"It is what it is. So is this the new *girlfriend* Mother insisted I meet?" The word "girlfriend" could have been replaced with "strumpet" from the way he said it.

Steve looked back and forth between her and Jack. Her tale of friendship was exposed for the lie it was, and he knew it. "It is. Becky, this is Jack. Jack, Becky McAllister."

"We've met. Went to school together if I remember correctly." And they'd done a whole lot more together that Becky didn't want to remember.

"It's about time you and Brad got here. Dinner is almost ready, and I don't like to be late," his mother said, coming to join them.

"Sorry, Mother. Traffic was bad." Always an excuse at the ready, he hadn't changed much from his high school days. "Brad will be right in. He had to take a call."

"I was just about to show Becky to the ladies' room. We'll both be right back." Steve grabbed her arm and tried to usher her past, but Jack stepped into their path.

"I'll show Becky the way since I need to go there myself. Give us a chance to get reacquainted. Steve can help Dad fix us a round of dinner drinks." He was all smiles to his mother, but Becky knew the black heart that beat in his chest.

"Good idea." His mother took Steve by the arm and pulled him toward the bar. "Run along, but hurry back."

Steve looked at her for confirmation, but it wasn't like she could say a word to stop what was unfolding. She followed Jack out of the room. It would be better if their confrontation wasn't in front of his parents, anyway.

"Fancy meeting you here—and with my brother. What game are you up to?" he snarled, grabbing her arm and turning her to face him.

"It's no game and none of your business. Steve and I are dating." She tried to stay strong, but the pressure of his grip had intensified.

"Does he know that you're the daughter of our housekeeper? You don't think he's serious about you, do you?" His lecherous grin shook her confidence, making her feel like she was eighteen again.

She hated that he had this hold over her and wished she could fight back, but as she stood there trembling, she knew she'd do no such thing. "He's not like you." *Well, almost nothing.*

"Have you told him anything?" Jack asked, leaning in closer, his cologne threatening to overpower her.

"No. There's nothing to tell, at least according to you and your blackmail demands. Besides, it's not like

I'm proud of who Byron's father is or that I foolishly believed your lies. So it would seem both of us have good reason for the secret to continue." It felt good to say what was on her mind for a change. Somehow, hanging around Steve seemed to have bolstered her confidence more than she knew.

He pulled her down to the end of the hall. "That's rich. A gold-digger like you won't give up easily once you've got your claws in him. I suggest you end it before I feel the need to warn my brother about you. Consider it another demand."

Becky was relieved when they reached the bathroom and he let her go. She slipped inside, not bothering to answer his new threat, anxious to get away from him. When she finished, she was equally pleased not to find him waiting and hurried back to the tearoom to find Steve.

She crossed the room to his side, unhappy to discover Jack was already back and talking to his brother. There was no way to know what lies the creep was spinning in her absence.

"Before we go to dinner, there's something I want to do," Steve said in a loud voice, garnering the attention of everyone in the room.

"What's going on?" his mother asked, pausing by the door and holding up the others from passing by.

Steve reached into his pocket and drew out a black box. *Oh my gosh. He's going to propose. Tonight?*

This she hadn't seen coming. Not by a long shot. Her heart raced as she glanced around the room. The shocked expressions on everyone's face echoed her own reaction.

Steve dropped to one knee and opened the box before taking her trembling hand in his. The solitaire diamond surrounded by tiny aquamarines sparkled up at her, the intricate setting so beautiful it took her breath away, robbing her of speech.

"Rebecca McAllister, even though we haven't known each other long, I do know I love you with my whole heart and soul. Will you do me the honor of becoming my wife?"

His mother's gasp was easily heard over the shocked silence of everyone else. "You can't be serious. You just met her. At a bar!" she exclaimed, not giving Becky the chance to answer. The derision in her voice had multiplied tenfold.

Becky still couldn't believe he'd just proposed. And used the L word. It wasn't real. That's what she had to remember. She took a deep breath, trying to calm her nerves.

"I am serious." Steve stood and drew her close, pulling her focus back to him and only to him.

"Will you marry me?" Steve's gaze never left her face, his eyes willing her to accept. Willing her to take the next step of their charade.

"Yes." Her voice came out low and soft, but everyone heard the word they didn't want to hear.

"I guess congratulations are in order," Judge Parker said, shaking Steve's hand. He gave Becky a stiff hug and a perfunctory kiss on her cheek, very much in keeping with what she expected from a disapproving parent keen on keeping up appearances. "Olivia, do the right thing and welcome Becky to the family."

His mother moved toward her, her chin rising several inches as she leaned in for an air hug. There'd be no loving mother-in-law relationship with this woman. "Congratulations," she uttered through tight lips.

"Congratulations." Brad stepped forward to give her a hug. At least his was real, not contrived like the others.

"Thank you." Becky smiled, gritting her teeth to help keep the false sentiment in place.

"Time to eat. We can talk more in the dining room," his mother ground out, turning on her heel and leaving the room.

They all followed, Steve's father clapping his son on the back as they entered the dining room ahead of her and Jack. "Congratulations, Becky."

Jack's voice held as much displeasure as his mother's, and when he stepped in to give her a hug, she stiffened. He held on a little too tight and a little too long for her liking. "Go through with this and I'll have your mother fired. Last warning," he whispered in her ear.

Becky had had just about enough of him. "Get your hands off me. And do what you want. By then, I'll be married to your brother, and you can't touch Byron or me. And my mother will quit if she finds out the truth, something I wish I had realized sooner." She might pay for her boldness later, but she'd deal with it, when and if it happened. It was as though the more power she took back, the more she wanted it.

Jack's eyes narrowed, his mouth curling up in a sneer. "Don't mess with me. You'll regret it."

Becky faltered a bit, her newfound confidence perhaps pushing Jack too far.

Steve came back to her side. "Everything okay here?"

"Yes, of course. Why wouldn't it be?" She pasted a smile on her face and gazed up at her new fiancé and then down at the gorgeous engagement ring he'd slid on her finger. It was beautiful, but surely it was as fake as the marriage would be. It made no sense for him to spend a fortune on something real, or at least she hoped it wasn't real. The mere idea of something this size and the value that would be associated with it would make her even more nervous just wearing it.

And if it were fake, there was the added bonus he might let her keep it when the marriage ended. A token of their time together.

Chapter Eleven

♥

STEVE HADN'T PLANNED TO ask Becky tonight, but something about Jack's presence and the perfect opportunity pushed him forward to make the proposal.

He'd known what to expect from his parents, but Jack was another story. His mother's cold indifference to anyone who crossed her path was a familiar tune. His father's patronizing gloating was the same, thinking marriage would destroy his career and ultimately prove him right and that it would be the final nail in Steve's run for the D.A.'s office.

But it was Jack's attitude toward Becky that left him reeling.

There was no love lost between the two, which had come as a relief, but it was the tension and fear that radiated from every pore of Becky's expression and actions since his brother walked in the door that left Steve in high-alert mode. Actually, thinking back, the change in her became obvious the minute his mother announced Jack was coming to dinner.

He did his best to run interference between the two of them, intentionally positioning them at the far end of the table. The whole marriage arrangement might be fake, but they were still friends—at least, he'd like to think they were. And part of being a friend involved protecting her from the likes of Jack.

The whole situation only served to confirm what he'd been thinking all along—Byron was Jack's son. He didn't need Becky to confirm or deny anything because the evidence was clear. Everything added up, except he didn't know why Jack hadn't acknowledged his son or done right by Becky. His brother was a selfish person and always had been, but this went way beyond that. And the bigger question—why was Becky determined to keep Jack's identity a secret?

He'd keep digging until he got the answers because Byron was his nephew. A nephew who was about to become his step-son and would gain the protection and benefits suited to him as a Parker. It was also a reason for them to stay together when the year was up. It was definitely something worth considering, since his worthless brother wasn't owning up to his mistakes and taking responsibility. The fact he cared about Becky only made it easier to make the leap.

His mother signaled for the wait staff to begin serving dinner and then called Randall over, speaking with him privately. After he left, she turned back to face everyone at the table. "Becky, why don't you tell us about yourself? I feel we should know more about who's joining our family."

Becky visibly shrank, as if preferring to stay unnoticed the entire meal. His mother's question was at least civil, her good graces mandating she make an effort.

Becky shot a quick glance at Jack before straightening in her seat and turning to his mother.

"As you know, I work at Charlie's, but I also have a son named Byron—he's five. I live with my mother and sister here in town."

His mother's eyes narrowed. "My son introduced you as a McAllister. That's not a common name. Any chance you're related to Judith McAllister?"

Becky blanched, her face pale. "Yes...that's my mother."

Steve knew that name from somewhere. He brushed it off as unimportant, assuming Becky must have said her name at one point or another.

His mother stood, barely controlled anger evident as she gripped the edge of the table. Something was wrong, and Steve had a bad feeling. The door to the kitchen opened, and one of the servants entered, moving to stand beside his mother. *Judith McAllister.* The housekeeper.

No way. He closed his eyes for a second, trying to digest this new information. Why hadn't Becky told him? He knew the answer, but it didn't make it any easier to process. She was embarrassed even though he'd already told her he didn't care. It was disappointing to realize she didn't believe him. Her mother's employer had zero effect on the marriage deal. Not that it wouldn't complicate things, but it didn't change their arrangement.

Becky spotted her mother, her eyes big as saucers, her mouth a tight line.

No one said a word, waiting for the inevitable and watching as the scene unfolded.

Steve started to rise, determined to protect Becky, but it was too late—Judith's gaze landing on her daughter. "Rebecca McAllister, what's the meaning of this? Why are you here?" Judith gazed around the table, taking note of everyone present.

"I'm sorry, Mother. This is Steve. Steve Parker. My boyfriend." Becky twisted the napkin in her lap as if she wanted to wring someone's neck. His? His mother's? Or Jack's? More than likely, the latter. Although he wasn't her boyfriend. He was her fiancé, something her mother would find out soon enough.

Her mother's gaze flicked in his direction but then returned to her daughter, the stiff set of her shoulders a good indicator of her barely concealed emotions. Complicated just got uglier. Becky hadn't told her mother the truth, either. In all fairness, he understood, given all the details.

"Did you know they were dating, Judith?" His mother's voice echoed disapproval.

"What's the big deal, Olivia?" The Judge finally spoke up, but Steve was sure his dismissal of his mother's outward contempt was based more on Steve ruining his run for office by getting involved with a woman, than it was out of concern for the newly engaged couple. His dad touted his title as youngest D.A. ever elected in the state of Texas status like it came with a crown. And he thought marriage and relationships were the sure-fire destruction to a man's career, solidifying his decision to divorce Steve's mother.

"The big deal is Becky's the housekeeper's daughter. Hardly suitable to become a member of the Parker family. Did you know, Judith?" His mother asked the question again, determined to get an answer.

Jack sat back, a wicked smile on his face as he enjoyed the show way too much for Steve's liking.

"No." Judith faced her employer, her normally calm demeanor shaken.

"Well, then how do you feel about your daughter getting engaged to my son?" His mother's thin-lipped smile didn't come close to reaching her eyes, the expression more distasteful in nature and a precursor of what was yet to come.

Steve had to put an end to this. "Mother, I don't think this is the time or place for this discussion. We weren't letting anyone know until we were sure, because of the publicity. The bottom line is Becky and I are engaged. Deal with it."

"You're engaged to Steve?" Judith shook her head, trying to process the information. He understood the position she was in and felt sorry for her. It was bound to be uncomfortable and finding out like this was less than ideal.

"Well, it's definitely not Jack. He knows his place," his mother snapped.

"I'm sorry, Mrs. Parker. I didn't know."

"We can talk about your employment Monday morning. That'll be all for tonight. You're dismissed." His mother's cold, sharp voice didn't bode well for Judith. It wasn't right that she should pay the price for the arrangement between him and Becky.

"I'll see you at home and we can discuss this." Judith's curt tone echoed the hurt written on her face. Her shoulders were slunk forward as she walked out of the room.

"You can't fire her for this," Becky said.

Steve wholeheartedly agreed. "Mother, you can't fire her. That's my fiancée's mother. Think of the bad press." He was trying to find something that would make her see reason, and the public eye was usually her Achilles' heel.

"Think of the bad press this is going to get anyway," she snapped. "You're marrying a girl and you didn't even know who her parents were. My housekeeper's daughter, nonetheless, and her father is unknown. I shudder to think of the women at the club and their laughter at my expense that I will have to suffer through." She shook her head, as if unable to comprehend the embarrassment he'd laid at her feet.

"I don't need to know her parents to know I love her. Look at Becky—she's agreed to marry me in spite of *my* parents." He couldn't believe he'd used the L-word. And more importantly, it sounded right, which didn't make any sense. He'd only known her a few weeks, but he'd loved every minute they were together. That's what he meant. *I love being with her, not that I love, love her.* It was just a slip of the tongue.

"Love is for fools," his mother quipped.

Becky jumped to her feet and raced out of the room to follow her mother.

"Amen to that. Probably the only thing Olivia and I ever agreed on," his father chimed in.

Jack pushed back from the table, an evil grin on his face. "Two weeks is hardly enough time to get to know someone. There's a lot you don't know about her, none of it good."

Steve stood, determined to go after Becky. "I know her quite well, and I've learned to trust in my own judgment." He stopped beside Jack and leaned down on the table, his face only inches from his brother's. "Anything in particular you want to tell the family?"

Jack's grin disappeared. His eyes darkened as he shook his head. "Nothing in particular, other than I think you're making a mistake. I went out with her a couple of times in high school. She was one of those girls always trying to trap a guy, but I saw right through her and dropped her shortly after."

"*Hmphh.* Apparently, you didn't drop her soon enough," Steve seethed through barely concealed anger.

Jack jumped to his feet, the two of them face to face. "What's that supposed to mean?"

"Nothing." Steve was furious, but he wasn't going to out Becky and Byron. Not without her permission and not until he knew why they were keeping it a secret. There was more to the situation, and Steve was determined to find out what.

Jack's confirmation he'd dated Becky stung. The timing was right, and Becky's visit to the house looking for Jack when she was desperate for money for Byron's surgery, all tied together in a neat package. Becky had lied to him directly when there was no reason for her to lie. None of which made any sense, except the money motive.

There are always two sides to every story.

What if Jack was telling the truth? Maybe Jack wasn't the father, and this was about getting the money she needed. For the first time, he began to doubt his own judgment. Jack was an idiot, something he'd always known. But Becky—he'd fallen for her story. Did that make *him* an idiot?

"Steve, wait. Before you go chasing after the girl, there's something else you should know," his mother called out to him.

He paused, torn between going after Becky and what his mother could possibly want to tell him that was urgent. Hopefully, she'd wait in the car and this would only take a few minutes.

"Three minutes, Mother."

"Fine. That's all it will take." She nodded toward the front room. "Follow me. What I have to say needs to be said in private."

Steve followed her, his curiosity ramping up into overdrive. He closed the door behind him and turned to face her.

"Okay, we're private. What's so important that it couldn't wait?"

"Normally, I wouldn't tell you this until after the wedding. But based on the short time you've known this girl and the fact I think you're making a huge mistake; I feel the urge to tell you what I set up years ago. You might want to rethink this marriage."

"Nothing you could tell me will change my mind. I love her." The words sounded more right every time he said them, but now wasn't the time to think on what that meant.

"This must remain confidential. Twenty years ago, I set up a large trust fund for you and your brother. The last thing I want is for Jack to get married to get his hands on the money and piddle it away."

"So when I get married, I have a trust fund?"

"Yes. Your father and I agreed and set them up long before the divorce. You'll get two million dollars transferred to your bank account as a wedding gift."

Steve was stunned. *Two million dollars.* Enough to cover the emergency fund for the Association before the other investors ponied up and in plenty of time to help the McDougall's. "That's quite generous. Thank you. But why the urgency to tell me now? I've got to go. Becky's upset, and I need to take her home."

"Think twice, Steve. About marrying her so quickly. She gets half the money if you do, unless you make her sign a prenup. Are you prepared to ask for one? To a girl with a background like that, there's no telling what she'll do, but I'm sure you'll come out the loser."

"Mother, you know nothing about her. It's my decision, and I'm marrying her whether you like it or not."

She shook her head and rolled her eyes, her frustration evident in the tense way she held her body.

"Night, Mother." Steve left the house to find Becky. He was thrilled his money issue would be settled, all the more reason to get married soon. They only had fourteen days to save the McDougall ranch.

Unfortunately, the seed of doubt had been planted. *Half the money.* It was true he'd been the one to approach Becky, and it was true she'd turned him down. But with two million dollars on the line, it was something he needed to take into serious consideration and think about a prenup. Even a fake marriage could come with a heavy price tag in this case when the wedding itself was real.

Chapter Twelve

♥

BECKY STOOD BY STEVE'S car, brushing away her tears, her whole body shaking. She spotted Steve running down the stairs toward where she waited. He pulled her into his arms and tilted her face up toward his, watching her close enough she couldn't hide her tears.

"Did you see my mother's face? I should have never agreed to this." Being in his arms helped more than it should, but she felt safe with him. Unfortunately, it didn't change what had just happened. Her stomach clenched in pain as the scene replayed in her head. Her mother's disappointment in her was the worst of it all.

"Why didn't you tell me the truth?" he asked, his voice gentler than she would have expected. He was always so understanding, even when he had every right to be upset with her.

All her good intentions of telling him tonight flew out the window. Her mother wasn't even supposed to be working. She could have faced off with Olivia Parker, but not with her mother standing there, her job in jeopardy and disappointment clearly etched on her face.

Her mother had always been there for her, even when she got pregnant not long after she'd turned eighteen. Her mother deserved better than this from Becky. And Steve had deserved the truth as well.

When will I learn? Secrets never ended well.

"I couldn't. It's complicated. I realized I needed to tell you right after we arrived. That's what I wanted to talk to you about. But then your mother interrupted us. And I'd hoped to tell my mother tonight as well, before the news of our engagement this weekend. You never told me you were going to ask tonight. I wasn't prepared."

"I had the ring, and the timing was perfect. Something about Jack's attitude toward you irritated me. As to telling your mother and me the truth, that's easy to say, hard to prove." His voice had an edge to it she didn't like. He'd never spoken to her like that before, and it left her reeling.

She'd ruined everything. "I'm sorry."

"When are you going to tell me the truth about Jack? That he's Byron's father. I don't deal well with lies. And although we're both entering into this marriage for our own reasons and it's temporary, I don't like to be blindsided."

Becky turned away. Could she trust him with the truth? He was a Parker first and would be her husband second. But he was also Byron's family. His uncle. And by the looks of things, Jack's threats of running her out of town on theft charges had evaporated, although her mother would still lose her job.

Lies kept destroying everything, and she wanted to come clean. "If I tell you the truth, will you promise not to tell anyone?"

"I promise, although I'm not sure I understand why you want it a secret." Steve held her gaze as if trying to understand her but unable to comprehend her request.

Trusting people didn't come easy to her, but it was time to trust Steve. "Let's just say no good can come of revealing his identity. It looks like my mother has already lost her job, and it's all my fault. I'm not sure how we are going to pay our bills or what we'll do, and I don't need more stress or problems."

"But Byron's father should be providing you with help. One of the big issues I've targeted in this state is to go after deadbeat dads and make them accountable. I can help you, but you have to let me."

"Even if it's your brother?" She'd never said those words to anyone else. What she hadn't expected was the barest hint of light reaching into her soul and turning into a glimmer of hope that one day things would be okay.

"Even more so if it's my brother." The steely resolve in Steve's voice was unmistakable. Integrity was one of the key character aspects of the man she appreciated, but this was more than she expected.

"What if I don't want help? What if I just want to be left alone to raise my son without interference?"

"There's a big difference between financial help and interference. And what about family? Byron's entitled to know his family and vice versa."

Steve had a point, and it was something she herself had thought about on several occasions. But then this was Jack they were talking about. And the Parker family. The only one Becky thought worthy of knowing Byron was Steve.

"I'm not sure his extended family would agree." She grimaced, recalling the scene at the dinner table.

"But they have the right to choose." Why was he pushing this? Was she just another cause of his, or did he really care? Or was it because of Byron?

"Jack is his father." She let out a breath at the words. It was as though saying them out loud purged her soul of the dark secret she'd been carrying around ever since she learned she was pregnant. The light burned brighter, but she didn't want anything to extinguish it. "But remember, you promised not to tell anyone. If I change my mind about that, I'll let you know, but for now, not a word."

Becky felt as though a huge weight had been lifted from her shoulders just by sharing her long-held secret. Her confidant was the least likely choice, but Steve was different. And she trusted him.

"Who else knows? Does Jack?" Steve ran a hand through his hair and shook his head, the tension in his body evident as he held himself rigid.

"Only you, Jack, and I know the truth."

"Your mother doesn't?" Steve frowned.

"Hardly. She wouldn't have remained working at your mother's if she knew the truth. We needed the income to make ends meet." There weren't many jobs in town, especially ones that paid as well as the affluent Parkers paid their staff. Discretion came with a price.

"You realize that makes him my nephew. And you never told me." Steve stated the obvious as though by saying it, it breathed life into the relationship. "And that day when you came to the mansion to talk to him—what is it you were after?" he asked, his even tones making her squirm under his direct gaze.

Becky felt like a client in his courtroom and not his fiancée—another difference between fake and reality. She knew what he was asking. "So now I'm a money-hungry floozy trying to suck your family dry for all it's worth?" Sarcasm at its finest, but it was her best defense. She shook her head, unable to believe how this evening had turned out. And she still had yet to face her mother. Tears ran down her cheeks unchecked.

"Hey now, I didn't say that." Steve's words couldn't undo what he'd already said. There was a reason she didn't trust people, and he'd just proven it.

"You might as well have. The deal's off. I'll find a way to take care of my son without Parker money." She ripped the ring off her finger and hurled it at him. "Take me home."

Maybe she'd regret the impetuous action later, like after she cooled down, but right now, it felt good to take years of pent-up anger out on someone—especially a Parker.

Steve bent down to retrieve the ring off the ground, staring hard at it as he turned it over and over. His gaze slid to her. "A deal's a deal. Byron still needs the surgery, and I still need you." His softly spoken words caused her to falter. She hadn't counted on him refusing to end the arrangement based on his beliefs.

"You need the poll ratings. Let's not confuse the facts. I can see the headlines now, D.A. Candidate and the Housekeeper's Daughter. That ought to sell some tabloids." She was desperately trying to hang on to her own beliefs that she was doing the right thing by ending it.

"Some things have changed, and we need to move up the wedding to next weekend." He spoke as if she hadn't just ended things, and his matter-of-fact tone told her he was serious. But next weekend? This was insane.

"I want to know why. The truth."

"You'll do it. You love Byron too much not to. As to why we need to move the wedding up, I just found out our wedding present comes in the form of two million dollars."

Two million dollars. More than Becky would ever see in this lifetime. And it was a wedding present. She took a deep breath, trying to calm the jackhammer pounding in her chest. "Two million?" she squeaked out.

"Yes. And I need some of the money ASAP. Some of that money will be yours." He grabbed her hand and placed the ring in her palm, closing her fingers over it. The edges of the diamond cut into her hand.

Without a word, she slid in the car. "What do you need the money for?"

Steve looked uncomfortable. "I can't say."

"Okay, then." She nodded. "What if I don't want your money?" It would be incredible to not have to worry about bills anymore, but she also had to be able to sleep with herself at night. It was one thing to do this fake marriage for Byron, quite another for her own personal gain. Apparently, that was Steve's specialty.

"It will be a part of the divorce settlement. You won't have a choice if you want a divorce."

"We'll see about that. I'll marry you in two weeks' time." It was still sooner than they'd originally planned, but Becky was determined to maintain some of the control. Especially given that he hadn't revealed why he wanted the money.

Steve drove back to her house, their confinement in the car magnifying the silence between them. Becky got out as soon as he pulled up to the curb in front of her house.

"I would like to meet your mother. Officially." Steve wasn't backing down, but neither was she. It might be true she had no choice but to go through with the deal, but it would be on her terms.

"No. Tonight I need to make amends. Alone."

"Fine. But, Becky, please meet me tomorrow morning at the park with Byron. We promised him, and I keep my promises."

She slammed the vehicle's door behind her, mentally preparing for the discussion with her mother. Guilt and worry caused her steps to slow. Becky pushed open the door to find her mother and sister sitting on the sofa, blank looks on their faces as if still in shock.

"I'm sorry, Mother." Becky raced across the room and dropped to her knees, grabbing her mother's hands in hers. "I should have told you, but I couldn't."

Her mother nodded. "Yes, you should have. We've always told each other everything, except about Byron's father—and now this. Somehow, I can't help but wonder if the two are related."

"I knew you would worry and wouldn't like it." Her mother had always been headstrong and protective of her and her sister, and if she knew the truth, there was no telling what her reaction would have been. Becky

didn't want her mistakes to be the downfall of her family.

"Worry? Who am I to stand in the way of love? If it's love." Her mother's gaze softened, and she turned her head to focus on Julia. "Can you go check on Byron and make sure he's asleep, please?"

"Not fair. I want to hear this." Her sister frowned, arms crossed in front of her chest.

"Except it doesn't concern you, and Becky's entitled to her privacy." Her mother's firm voice managed to elicit the desired response as her sister got to her feet.

"Fine." Julia left the room, the sixteen-year-old pout on her face not becoming. In some ways, she was still a child.

"It is love, isn't it?" Her mother held one finger under Becky's chin, forcing her to make eye contact. It was one of the ways her mother used when she was growing up to elicit the truth. This close, it was hard to lie. But she couldn't tell her she was getting married for Byron's sake. Her mother wouldn't allow it, and she'd been sworn to secrecy with Steve. She owed him that much, even if he was a jerk at times.

"It happened fast. I feel things I've never felt before." At least that was the truth. She liked Steve. A lot. She even thought she might have been falling for him until he accused her of being a gold-digger. Although in truth, he hadn't said it in so many words, just asked her motives. It was all so confusing.

"Is he Byron's father?"

"What? No, Mother. He's not." At least not everything she said was a lie.

"I'm disappointed you didn't tell me what was going on, but I love you, and I want what's best for you. If you want to marry Steve Parker, then you should. Far be it for me to stand in the way. I'll find another job, don't worry. Olivia Parker's been good to me but always because I've not overstepped my bounds. She won't let this one go." Her mother patted her hand, a gentle smile of reassurance on her face.

"I'm sorry, Mom. I'll make sure you and Julia are taken care of. I promise." It might take some renegotiation with Steve, but it was something she was willing to do. After all, in a way, he was also responsible for her mother's termination come Monday morning.

Chapter Thirteen

♥

THE EXTRA WEEK BEFORE the wedding was problematic but not anything Steve couldn't handle. Olivia Parker was stubborn, snobbish, and unreasonable, just like his father, but she would pay out the trust fund as promised. Marriage or no marriage.

Steve had often wondered where he fit in with the family because he certainly wasn't like them. He still couldn't believe it when she'd told him she fired Judith McAllister. At least she'd given the poor woman a severance check considering the twenty-plus years she'd worked for the family. His mother did have a heart, even if it was a small one. He only hoped it was a sizable amount because jobs in Riverbend were few and far between.

Knowing he'd soon have the trust fund, Steve was willing to put up his own money to expedite the Mc-Dougall payment, preferring to be on the safe side of the deadline.

Avoiding his mother and her disapproving gazes, he headed into town bright and early to pick up Becky and Byron. Today, he was taking them to the city. Away from prying eyes. A place where they could tap back into some of the fun and laughter he'd grown to enjoy around them and wanted back desperately.

She had every right to be upset with him. For a person who earned a living by using good word choices, he'd done a lousy job questioning Becky about Byron's parentage, doubting her. He should have trusted his gut instincts, something he'd done in the past with success. This time he'd failed, and he knew the reason why. *Jack*.

Steve didn't like the idea of his brother and Becky together, and it had cost him the voice of reason in his head. And there was only one reason he'd be jealous of Jack—he cared about Becky. More than he'd planned or expected to care about anyone.

Thankfully, she agreed to give him another chance. And today, he wanted to prove to her it had been the right decision.

He spotted Becky and Byron sitting on the front porch as he pulled up in front of her house. Apparently, he wouldn't be meeting her mother this morning. He wasn't sure why the idea bothered him, but today wasn't the day to press the issue.

"Mr. Steve, you came." Byron ran forward when Becky let go of his hand.

Moving around to the passenger side, he knelt next to Byron to return the young boy's enthusiastic greeting with a warm hug. "Good morning, buddy. You ready to have some fun today?" He ruffled the boy's hair.

"Yup. Sure am." Byron's wide grin tugged at Steve's heart.

"Good morning, Becky," Steve said, leaning down to drop a kiss on her cheek. It would be expected, but he didn't want to push his luck. Not yet, anyway.

She stiffened, but otherwise, there was very little reaction to the casual observer or to any media hounds if they were lurking about anywhere. "Good morning. What do you have in mind for today?"

"I thought we'd head to Onalaska. There's a great beach there where the Trinity River opens up to the lake. I've got a picnic basket filled with lots of good food. And I have a blanket. The only thing I couldn't rustle up was some toys for Byron on such short notice."

Becky smiled. "I think we have that covered. Byron, run upstairs and grab your football and bag of sand toys while I move your car seat."

"Okay, Mommy. This is going to be so much fun. I'm a good ball thrower, Mr. Steve. You just wait and see." The kid took off before Steve had a chance to answer.

He shot Becky a questioning glance, the obvious elephant from Byron's innocent comment hanging between them.

"He is a good ball thrower. Must be genetics, but not something I would take from him. I like to think I'm more accepting of my son's talents no matter what they are."

"Great attitude. Just for the record, football is not one of my hidden talents, trust me."

"Good. I rather like knowing that, to tell you the truth. Reminds me how different you and Jack are, which is definitely a positive."

"Listen, before we go any further, I want to apologize for my behavior and comments the other day. I wasn't thinking clearly, and I let it cloud my judgment. I trust you, which is a good thing considering we're going to be married." He smiled, hoping to encourage her to accept his apology.

"Thank you. It hurt, but I'm glad we've cleared the air. Especially since, like you said, we're getting married." Becky grinned, and suddenly, the awkwardness had vanished, her light teasing more than welcome.

He stepped in close, deciding there was no time better than the present to seal the return to normalcy between them. With a real kiss—not a peck on the cheek.

Steve leaned down and dropped a kiss on her lips, lingering a few moments to savor the feel of her mouth. Warm and perfect. Just like her.

"I got them!" Byron shouted as he came running out the front door, ending the kiss.

They drove to the lake, Steve relieved to have escaped media attention. The last thing he wanted was for photographers to be hanging around while he was trying to have fun with his soon-to-be new family. This time was just for them.

The weekend had been all that he could have hoped for, especially the day at the beach. Byron, it turned out, did have a great throwing arm—for a four-year-old, that was. He was also a good runner, their game of chase proving that. Byron played in the sand, letting the grown-ups talk. He and Becky were back on the same page, and as if by mutual agreement, they didn't discuss his family or their displeasure with the engagement. It's not as though what they thought mattered.

And if Becky's kiss goodbye was any indication, she'd completely forgiven him. A kiss caught by a persistent photographer who'd followed them around at a reasonable distance ever since spotting them at a restaurant Saturday evening. Then Sunday had plenty of photographers, and, of course, Byron ate up the attention. What kid didn't like the idea of having his picture in the paper?

The drive to Houston took a little over two hours, the traffic heavier than normal. The Houston Texans must have had a home game. Steve never had time to get into football, preferring the library and law books to jocks and egos. Not even when his own brother had tried to go pro could he get into the game.

Inside his apartment, Steve loosened his tie, ready to unwind. He pressed the Do Not Disturb button on his phone. Ever since the media had gotten wind of his engagement, the phone hadn't stopped ringing with either congratulations or reporters wanting to get the scoop.

He'd tried to prepare Becky for the onslaught, but after years of handling them, he knew it wouldn't be easy for her. He hated having to be away from her all week, but at least she promised to call if things got rough. The one good thing that had come from all of it was that they were back on the same team, partners in crime, but it also left him wondering if he should go through with the wedding. Once upon a time not long ago, it wouldn't have mattered if they got married. They both stood to gain something. But now, caring about her the way he did, made him question his actions and the problems she would face as a result of being associated with him. *Her quiet life was a thing of the past.*

Except now, there were two million other reasons to go through with it. And saving the McDougall property wasn't something he could walk away from. He'd made it his personal mission to help, and now it was within reach. And after learning the truth about Byron, it made it even more imperative to marry Becky, if for no other reason than to give his nephew the Parker name. The marriage was a temporary price to pay for doing good in the community, and Steve couldn't turn his back on the ranchers and farmers *or* his nephew.

The following morning, Steve gathered his briefcase and headed for the office. Between his caseload and the campaign, things were in full swing, and he had tons to do if he intended to get back to Riverbend this weekend. Even though they were only doing a Justice of the Peace wedding, they still needed to coordinate their schedules and figure out what happened after the wedding, including finding a place to live. The element of realism would be lost if they didn't live together.

Steve would still have to commute back and forth to the city, but he was looking forward to spending more time with Becky. Being with her this past weekend, he'd come to the realization that he fully believed her about Jack and her story. She might not be willing to tell him why she wanted to keep Byron's parentage a secret, but then he wasn't willing to tell her why he needed the money. Both had their secrets, but Steve trusted her, much the same way she trusted him.

They were in this together.

It was incredible to know he had a nephew, and the more he'd spent time with Byron this weekend, the more he'd grown to love the kid. Steve knew no matter what happened in the future between him and Becky, he wasn't willing to let Byron fade out of his life. And as to Becky's decree that he not breathe a word about her admission, he would honor that promise.

But it wouldn't stop him from putting the heat on Jack to do what was right by Becky and Byron, and without a blood test, the only way to do that was to get Jack to admit the truth on his own.

Steve walked into his office building. People were everywhere, phones ringing off the hook. Several calls of congratulations rang out as he crossed the room to his office. He hadn't even had time to take off his coat and sit down before Harry flew into his office. "I didn't realize campaign managers showed up before nine a.m.," Steve said, unable to resist harassing the man. "What's the occasion? There seems to be quite a buzz in the room." Not that he didn't already know, but where was the fun in that?

"What? You're asking me what? Why haven't you been answering your phone? I've been trying to reach you." Harry was agitated, and maybe rightfully so, but Steve hadn't felt like returning his calls, knowing what he'd walked into this morning.

"I turned it off. I was exhausted and needed some sleep."

Harry shook his head. "I can't believe you took my advice and got engaged. But whatever it is you think you're doing here, guess again. I want you to go back to Riverbend. *Today*. The public is eating this up. Hot-shot D

.A. candidate engaged to housekeeper's daughter. How did you manage to pull something like this off? It's exactly the publicity boost we needed."

He hoped Becky didn't see the tabloid or she'd be upset all over again. She knew they'd plaster that one little fact all over the headlines. "I didn't plan anything. And why does everyone care what her mother's job is?" For him, this had been about poll ratings, helping Becky, and more recently, funding the emergency account for the Tumble County landowners.

"Are you kidding? It's the story of Prince Charming coming to the rescue of a poor maiden. You know, like a modern-day Cinderella. Your numbers have skyrocketed." Harry looked like he was about to explode with excitement.

"Can't we downplay the mother's role? The poor woman got fired."

"Downplay? No way! This is rich. Talk about the publicity. People will rally behind you for sticking by the woman you love over your own mother. True love wins it all. The sympathy votes will roll in."

"I wish voters would pay more attention to my record than the Prince Charming aspect." Steve shook his head, letting out a deep sigh of frustration. Yes, he'd signed on for it, but a big part of his reason had been to help Becky and, in doing so, help himself.

"Too late for that. And I intend to use every avenue I've got to see that you win. It's my job." Harry grinned, all too pleased with the turn of events. "I want you to go back to Riverbend. Take your files or whatever you need and work from home. We need to keep you and Becky on the front page of the news, not buried on page ten in a tiny corner."

"But I just got back here, and I have a lot to do." As much as he liked the idea of seeing Becky again, he wasn't liking the idea of using her for career advancement. *At least, not anymore.*

"Look, this is your chance to win. You've got a laptop— use it. Get your secretary to reschedule meetings. When's the wedding? Hopefully, not until after the election."

"You'll be disappointed, then. It's in two weeks." Steve was grateful they'd already decided on a date knowing it would help put an end to the media madness.

"That's preposterous. How can you put together a wedding in two weeks? It takes months."

"It's called a Justice of the Peace at City Hall. Probably my father, as luck would have it." Steve laughed, knowing each drop of information was bringing Harry closer to the brink of having a fit as he tallied up the lost votes.

"No. No. No. That won't do. Your fiancée agreed to this? What's going on?" His eyes narrowed suspiciously. "You go home, meet someone, and a couple of weeks later, you get engaged and tell me you're doing a whirlwind wedding. It doesn't add up. What gives? I know you better than to believe all this." Harry plopped down in the seat in front of the desk and leaned back, his hands behind his neck.

"It's called love." Steve laughed and moved to sit down behind his desk. "You said *get married,* so I am." He wasn't about to tell him the rush came in the form of much-needed money.

"Whatever you say." He shook his head. "Just get back to Riverbend. Please. Don't forget, I've got a lot riding on your election, too."

"I'll go back, but only because I want to see my fiancée and you won't be hounding me to get back to Houston."

Harry laughed. "I'll hound you if you come back here."

It was a good thing he was his own boss and could make his own decisions because he liked the idea of going back to Riverbend for the next couple of weeks. It would give him time to rent a house, the idea of staying with his mother beyond a couple of days as unsettling as losing the election. It didn't take long before he worked out the details with his secretary, stopped at the house for more clothes, and was back on the road to Riverbend.

And Becky. The idea put a smile on his face and warmth in his heart.

An hour and a half later, he pulled into the driveway of his mother's house and was greeted by Randall. "Good to see you again, sir." The older man took his garment bag and headed up the grand staircase.

"Thanks. Good to see you, too." Steve nodded.

"Who is it, Randall?" his mother called from down the hall.

He paused, leaning over the banister to answer. "Steve has returned, madam." The old coot barely moved his lips as he spoke before continuing on his way.

"Steve?" His mother joined him in the foyer.

"Hello, Mother. I came back to see Becky and look for a place to live, so I hope you don't mind me returning so soon." Steve gave her a perfunctory hug, one they'd perfected over the years to give the illusion he was a loving son happy to see his mother.

Her smile disappeared at the mention of Becky. "Nonsense. You've always been welcome here. You've just always made it a point to stay away, so pardon my surprise. Why the rush to find a place to live? You've got lots of time, and you can just stay here."

"We've decided to get married in City Hall a week from this Friday." It was the first time he'd managed to render his mother speechless, her shocked expression priceless.

"That's ridiculous. My son, married at City Hall? I won't stand for it. You're not a commoner."

"I want to marry the woman I love, Mother. That's all that matters. I see no reason to wait." It was the second time he'd said the words, each time sounding more and more familiar on his lips. Was it possible he was falling for Becky? It wasn't part of their deal, but it seemed inevitable on his part. What was there not to love? That was the question.

His mother snorted derisively, lines of tension on her face. "That's just it. I don't think you love the girl." Her steely gaze bore into his, trying to read his response. He'd learned a long time ago not to react.

"And why, then, would I be marrying her?"

"I don't know. Poll ratings, perhaps?" His mother was a sharp old bird, but there was nothing she could legally do to stop him from getting married, regardless of the reason he was doing it.

He wouldn't fall into the trap of admitting anything. "You have it all wrong. Once upon a time, you met Dad and fell in love. It happens."

"I met, thought I was in love, got pregnant, got married, got divorced. Not a great story."

"Well, then, at least Becky's not pregnant. Our story will end differently than yours."

"I'm not a fool, and I hate to see you throw your life away. You know, for all that you assume I don't care about you, it's simply not true. I was just never good with kids." His mother fixed a cocktail and came to sit beside him.

"Let's hope you've improved with time because Byron will soon be your grandson." Already was, but Steve wasn't about to split hairs or break Becky's confidence.

"Step-grandson, and don't remind me." She curled her lip up disdainfully, turned, and made her way across the room, stopping to turn back when she reached the door. "You're making a big mistake. I thought you were smarter than that." His mother walked out of the room, determined to have the last cutting words.

Chapter Fourteen

♥

BECKY LOOKED UP AS the bell over the restaurant door jingled. *Steve.*

Her heart beat a little faster as she watched her handsome fiancé walk across the room toward her. Pretend fiancé, yes, but the fluttering in her stomach was all too real. She liked him, more than she should, and that was information she'd keep to herself. They had an agenda, and she'd stick to it, just like she'd promised.

"Hey there," he said as he slid into his favorite booth in her section.

She laid his menu down. "Hi to you, too. I thought you were in Houston. What brings you back here so soon?" There was no disguising her surprised pleasure at seeing him, but hopefully, he didn't read too much into it.

"I had to come back to take care of some things, and I was worried about you and the publicity attached to our engagement. I knew it would be a bit overwhelming." His gaze lingered on her as if reassuring himself she was handling things okay.

Another sign of what a caring person he was. "That's sweet of you. There has been a steady stream of people calling my phone, and a few have come to town, but there's not much to tell, so they leave quick enough." Their engagement was big news, but Becky wasn't much of a talker and had no intention of talking to the press other than to confirm the relationship.

"I'm relieved to hear it. Sometimes being under the microscope is stressful." He sat back in the booth but continued to study her. There was something different in his gaze, but she brushed it off. They both had a lot going on.

Becky laughed. "The locals who come in here stare, dying to ask me questions, but most don't. I figure they're waiting on me to do the talking. So, what do you want for lunch? The special and a glass of sweet tea?" She moved on to a safer subject.

"Am I that predictable?" He smiled.

"When it comes to food, yes. Everything else, no." She grinned and turned to leave.

"Becky?" he called out after her. She turned around and returned to the table.

"Change your mind? Going to step outside your comfort zone?" she teased.

"No. At least not with food. But with you, yes. I was thinking we should spend time together this week. As in a lot of time. Not just for the publicity, but for us. If we're going to be living together, I think we should get to know each other better."

"I think it makes perfect sense. Tonight?"

"That would be great. Anything to be out of my mother's house."

"What are you, sixteen?"

"Sometimes around her it feels like it." He laughed. "Maybe we could check out a movie at the theater with Byron. I noticed *Mary Poppins* was playing."

"*Um*, that's a little old for a five-year-old. But you're in luck, *Happy Feet* is playing, too, and he'll love it."

"I've got a lot to learn, don't I?"

"You do but give it time. Pick us up at five-thirty, and we can stop at the hot dog stand for some chili-cheese dogs and fries. Make it an old-fashioned, honest-to-goodness date."

"You're on."

Steve polished off his lunch, letting her know he had work to do while in town. When he was finished, he headed her way. Mindless of anyone who might be watching, he pulled her in his arms and kissed her. And not just any goodbye kiss, a kiss that also managed to say, *I can't wait to see you again*. A kiss that left her breathless.

"See you tonight, beautiful." He grinned. Too bad it was all an act because there was no faking her racing heart. The man had quite an impact on her.

Her shift took forever, but when it was over, she rushed to pick up Byron from school. After parking the car, she made her way to his classroom just as the bell rang.

Byron spotted her and came running up to show her the popsicle stick craft he'd made today. "Look, Mommy. I made it for you. It's a box for special things, like jewelry and stuff." He beamed.

"I love it. Thank you, honey." She kissed the top of his head, treasuring his gift. She signed her name on the pick- up sheet and then headed back to the car, the two of them walking hand in hand. "Guess what? I've got good news."

"Are we getting a dog?" Poor kid still hadn't given up on pushing for one every chance he got.

"No. Better. Mr. Steve is back in town and taking us for hot dogs. And then Steve and I are going to the movies for some grown-up time. You can play with Julia."

"Yay! I like Mr. Steve. A dog would be nice, too. Don't forget, you told me one day I could have one. Maybe tomorrow will be the day," he said, his eyes lit with excitement.

"Not tomorrow. Let's just concentrate on dinner first."

"Okay, Mommy. I like the movies, too, but I don't want to watch all the mushy stuff if you two are going to kiss." Byron scrunched up his face in distaste. "And Aunt Julia promised she'd watch *Toy Story* with me tonight."

"If you're sure." This evening had just turned into an unsupervised date. A real date—the idea leaving her breathless.

Becky drove back to the house, ignoring her son's comment about the kiss. She helped Byron out of his car seat, and they headed inside, Byron dropping his book bag by the door.

"Not so fast, young man. Run upstairs and put away your book bag and then come back down. We need to clean up a few things before we go. It's our turn."

"Okay." Chores weren't his favorite thing to do, but Becky tried to make it fun by doing them with him and making a game of it. Her mother had done the same with her and it had worked wonders. But then, Becky figured her mother would know better than anyone considering she was a professional housekeeper.

She barely had time to finish getting ready when Steve knocked at the door. "Hi, there. You look nice," he said, kissing her openly in front of a wide-eyed Byron. "Ready to go, buddy?"

"Yeppers." He took Steve's hand as they stepped off the porch and made their way to the car. Becky wasn't used to competing for Byron's attention, the gesture both off- putting and welcome at the same time. She wanted her son to like and respect Steve, and as for Steve, he would be an excellent role model for Byron.

Steve drove to the hot dog joint and pulled into a drive- thru spot, rolling down his window to place the order.

"Just a plain hot dog with catsup for Byron. And a sweet tea. I'll take a fully loaded house special." She grinned.

"Living dangerously, aren't you?"

"How's that?"

"Between the spicy chili and onions, those are re- served for stomachs of steel, last I checked."

"Still are." She laughed. "My mother cooks with heavy spices and I've gotten used to the heat."

"Good to know." He placed their orders, adding his own.

"You and Byron have something in common. You both like plain and simple."

"There's nothing wrong with just chili and mustard. I like to keep my stomach in one piece."

"Wait till I cook for you at home." It sounded intimate and genuine, like they were a real couple, something she was getting used to far more than she should, but it felt nice. Sweet. The one thing she hadn't factored in their plans was her falling for Steve. She'd have to be careful or, by the time the year was out, he'd break her heart.

"I'm looking forward to it. Just remind me to hide the hot sauce." His cheeks dimpled, his teasing finding the mark.

"Be careful not to get catsup on Mr. Steve's seats. Make sure it all gets in your mouth."

"Yes, ma'am," Byron said, his muffled words proof he was getting at least some of it in his mouth. Clean seats were more important than manners at the moment, so she'd let that one slide.

Steve handed him extra napkins from the bag. "Don't worry, buddy, leather seats clean easy, and here's extra napkins."

"Thanks, Mr. Steve. But I'll be super careful, any-way."

"Good deal." He smiled, taking another bite of his own hot dog.

"Nice and spicy, just like I wanted," she said, dabbing the corners of her mouth with her own napkin.

"Just wait till you throw ice cream in the mix. You might not be so happy." Steve shot her a challenging look, daring her to correct his assessment.

"You didn't say we were going for ice cream after."

"I love ice cream," Byron said. "I can mix my dinner with ice cream and my belly will say yummy."

Steve laughed. "Mine, too. And for the record, I was trying to surprise Byron. Didn't realize ice cream had to come with a warning."

"Now you do. But based on the time, it will have to wait until another outing. We don't want to be late for the movie, which by the way has been upgraded to *The Wedding Planner*. Byron already had plans with Julia, so we need to drop him off at the house after dinner."

Steve nodded. "Perfect movie, don't you think?" His mischievous grin made her more nervous.

"*Aww*, darn it. Ice cream sounded good," Byron said, leaning forward in his seat.

"I'll tell Julia you can have some."

"Yeah!" Byron shouted, happy once again.

Steve started the engine and drove back to her house. Becky took him inside, filling Julia in with all the instructions for the evening.

Five minutes later, they arrived at the movie theater. This was the first time they were going on a date-date. Just the two of them as a real couple. Becky's breath hitched when Steve took her hand and led her toward the entrance.

The marquis was a symbol of the days when it first opened. The letters were still manually changed to announce the three movies. Becky loved *The Wedding Planner*, having seen it three times already, but she couldn't imagine Steve going for it. Most people viewed it as a chick flick.

"Two tickets, please," he said, pulling out his wallet.

Becky started to dig in her purse, feeling it was only right she pay for her entry.

He put out his hand to stop her. "I've got this." Steve winked, his message clear. They were on a date, and in his world, the man paid. Fine. Chivalry wasn't dead in her books, not to mention the expense wasn't in her monthly budget.

"Popcorn?" he asked, stopping in front of the counter.

"No, thanks. We just ate." Becky was full, but she also didn't want him paying the exorbitant prices for movie theater food after having bought the tickets.

Steve led her into the theater, the lighting dim but still enough to see where they were going. There weren't many people here, leaving their seat choices wide open. "You okay with sitting in the middle?"

She shrugged. "Let me guess, they're a good place to be seen?" Her normal was in the back row. Who was she kidding? It had been a long time since she'd been to the theater and, therefore, nothing about it was normal.

"Actually, I was thinking we would see it better. Kind of in your face and more real."

His answer surprised her because it meant he wanted to see the movie. Steve Parker had a romantic side, whether he wanted to admit it or not. "Sounds good." She'd sit anywhere he wanted as long as it was with him.

Once seated, he leaned in close. "I've seen this before, but I like it. It's pretty funny if you ask me. All the things that can go wrong, do." He lowered his voice as another couple came and sat at the end of the row.

"I agree. I've seen it three times, but it never gets old."

Steve took her hand as the light darkened, and the previews flashed across the screen.

"We should go see that one. What do you think?" he asked after the preview for another law enforcement versus alien finished.

More along the lines of what she expected from a guy, but still, not what she would have thought the city attorney would choose. Went to show how wrong you could be about someone. Or how right. The man she'd agreed to marry was a down-to-earth nice guy. Real.

Throughout the movie, he held her hand, commenting on some of her favorite parts. It was as though he could read her mind. Shoulder to shoulder, he leaned closer, Becky inhaling his cologne, the woodsy spice making her want to snuggle in his arms in front of a warm fire.

By the time the movie was over and the credits were rolling, Becky was forced to admit the truth.

The arrangement was temporary, but she wasn't sure she wanted it to end. Against all odds, she'd fallen for Steve—something she'd have to deal with later. For now, she wanted to enjoy his company and the wonderful feeling that came with being treated as though he cared.

As his someone special.

His soon-to-be wife.

Chapter Fifteen

♥

THE WEEK SPED BY fast, whether because his days were filled with work or his nights were filled with fun, he wasn't sure. And for the first time in his life, he questioned his goals and some of the decisions he'd made in the past. It made no sense, but it was almost as if the fun nights and being around Becky made the days lighter, less stressful, his focus on the *end* of the day for a change. Not how to take on more work.

Pizza night at Becky's had been relaxing. He'd enjoyed getting to know her mother and sister and hearing some of the stories of Becky growing up. And he loved to see her blush. But the most fun had been the night they played Twister. Byron and Julia had a great time, but no more so than he had. Games hadn't been a part of his childhood, and although at first it had been hard to loosen up, it hadn't taken long to get into the spirit of the game.

Every round, it seemed, brought crazier positions than the last. A few, however, weren't so much crazy as they were an awareness factor. Of Becky. A few times, he hadn't been able to resist teasing her with a kiss, much to the delight of Byron and her sister.

Judith McCallister, on the other hand, just grinned and nodded, a silly smile on her face as though she were privy to some secret information. Long after Byron had gone to bed, they'd stayed up and talked, joked, and laughed. Something else he'd never done growing up. It was like being part of a family.

Steve was afraid to admit it out loud, but he was looking forward to tying the knot with Becky next week and moving into their new house. Yes, he'd have to return to the city, but he'd find a way to be home more, wanting to enjoy every minute of his new family for as long as they were in his life.

A part of him wished he'd organized a more traditional wedding, but on such short notice, a judge was the best he could do. Even the upcoming election didn't excite him as much as it once had, knowing the responsibilities would keep him away longer. It was like Becky and Byron had some secret scent they wore that kept him coming back for more. More love and laughter. More family.

He made his way downstairs to the breakfast table. There were a lot of last-minute details with the house that needed tending to before he brought his bride home.

"We need to talk," his mother said, surprising him once again that she was up and about this early in the morning.

"If it's about the wedding, there's nothing to talk about."

"Don't get smart with me. You need to hear me out."

"Fine, Mother. What is it you want to say?"

"I want to offer you an alternative to marriage." His mother didn't give up easily, a trait he inherited when he wanted something bad enough.

"What's that supposed to mean?" So much for casual.

"Call off the engagement and I'll release your trust fund now, without the marriage clause, and add a million-dollar bonus. You're smart with your money, not like your brother. I'm sure you could handle it."

Nothing could have surprised him more, but then it shouldn't have. It came down to the money or him marrying someone she considered unacceptable. But still, he had no words.

"You won't need to marry beneath your station or in haste. My one condition is a public breakup so that everyone knows the truth. No speculation. I want an end to this nonsense." She paused, clearly studying him for a reaction, but he offered none. "I'll give you five minutes to decide."

Steve thought hard, the seconds ticking loudly on the grandfather clock against the wall. *Three million dollars.* Calling that a lot of money was an understatement. But if they didn't get married, he ran the risk of poll ratings dropping. They say money couldn't buy happiness, and whoever said it was right—at least in his case. His happiness would come from winning the election and being an advocate for others. Yes, the McDougalls needed the money, but he wasn't sure it would buy their happiness. They only wanted their son back, something money couldn't do.

What his mother didn't understand was that the money only reinforced his decision to go through with the marriage. But it was his increasing poll ratings that drove him the most. No amount of bonus money could offset the position he'd get when the election results posted.

Plus, there was the thought of losing Becky... "No deal," he said.

His mother shook her head. "And here I thought you were the smart one. No good will come of this, mark my words."

"I know what you're trying to do, but you're wrong. I want to marry Becky and look forward to having Byron as my stepson. I might even adopt him."

His mother bristled, her back ramrod straight. "Ruin your life, then. I wash my hands of you."

"Now that we've established my motives are pure, any chance you could give us our wedding present a few days early? I've got some special things I need to take care of, and it would be a huge help."

"Fine. What does it matter now, anyway? But there will be no bonus, of that you can be certain."

"I wouldn't expect otherwise. Thank you, Mother."

"I'll have the money transferred to your account. Now, go away. My head hurts as much as my heart."

"Dramatics don't suit you, Mother. It'll be fine. You'll see." Fine as far as he was concerned, anyway. His mother had always had high hopes for him, but apparently, it didn't include anything that would besmirch her public appearance. And marrying the housekeeper's daughter certainly did that. "Becky's a nice girl. I'll let you in on a little secret to help you deal with this. The rush on the wedding is because Byron needs surgery, and he'll be added to my insurance plan, which is far better than the policy she has."

"Then just pay for her share. You don't have to do this."

"That's not why I'm marrying her, only expediting it." He didn't want his mother to think badly of Becky, and telling her the truth was important.

"What's wrong with the boy?"

"That would be confidential information and not something I'm willing to share. Not so you and your gossipy friends can sit around and chat about it."

"Fine. It's your money. Spend it however you want. But I think it's foolish for you to pick up the tab on someone else's kid." So much for appealing to her nice side.

"Goodbye, Mother." He stood and left the room, biting back the retort that sprang to his lips. That kid, as she referred to Byron, was her grandson. Her *blood*. If only she knew the truth...but the truth wasn't his secret to reveal.

Chapter Sixteen

♥

BECKY STILL COULDN'T BELIEVE she was getting married tomorrow. She didn't feel any different, other than secretly having feelings for her soon-to-be fake husband. But then there would be no beautiful white gown, no decorated church, no floral bouquets or bridesmaids. Just the judge at City Hall. Nothing special. Just like their marriage would be, for as long as they needed it.

Kayla was going to be her witness and planned on showing up first thing in the morning to help with her hair. It would be the closest she felt to being a bride. She wouldn't even have a brand new dress. It seemed silly to buy one for a ten-minute ceremony only a handful of people would see.

Becky finished checking and refilling condiments on the tables in her section at Charlie's after a few of her customers had finished lunch and left. It was a light day, tips even lighter. She tried not to think about it. Byron's surgery would be paid for, and that's what she needed to focus on.

The bell over the door jingled, and she instinctively looked up to see who the customer was. *Steve.* Her heart did an extra beat as he waved to Katie and made his way to his usual booth in her section.

"Hiya, stranger," she said. "What brings you here today?" She grinned, handing him a glass of iced tea made just the way he liked it. Half sweet, half unsweet.

"There's a certain blonde I can't get enough of, truth be told." He winked.

"That's good, all things considered." Becky glanced down at the engagement ring on her finger. It was more than she would have normally ever chosen for herself, but she loved it. Becky had never told Steve her birthday, so he must have asked her mother or sister. Either that or he was just plain lucky. She still couldn't believe it was real.

"The special?" Becky asked, offering him the menu but fully expecting him not to take it. Like usual.

"Of course. I was in town to handle some things at the house and needed lunch."

She slid the menu back into her apron pouch. "You've been here every day this week. People will talk." She grinned.

"Let them." He squeezed her hand and grinned back. She loved the little crinkles at the corners of his eyes when he smiled. For however long they were married, she intended to make the most of it. It might be the only chance she got if Prince Charming never planned on showing up.

"I'll be back with your meal shortly." She headed to the kitchen, turning in the order.

She rang out a few customers, listening for her order to be called when it was done. It didn't take long, and Becky did a pickup and headed back to Steve's table.

He was on the phone, deep in conversation. "Hang on a second," he said, lowering the phone from his ear.

She placed the plate of spaghetti in front of him and refilled his tea. "Do you need anything else?"

"Nothing, thanks," he said and pointed at his phone. Steve was eager to get back to his call, so she walked away.

Becky wondered who he was talking to so intently. Call it curiosity or being nosey, it didn't matter. She was marrying the man tomorrow and deserved to know everything about him that she could in such a short amount of time.

"Okay, just let me know." She walked away but hovered close by, wiping down a couple of tables and straightening the napkins and condiments. Eavesdropping might be wrong given their situation, but she did it anyway.

"I got the money yesterday, and it should be transferred into your account later today. Then we can put some closure to the McDougall deal once and for all." Steve spoke into the phone, keeping his voice low, but not low enough. He obviously wasn't aware she was wiping down the table behind him.

"Yes." He nodded, responding to whatever was being said on the other end of the call. "Let's find out who's next up on the chopping block and figure out what we can to expedite settling the matter."

Becky winced. It sounded like Steve was involved with men forcing the foreclosures and buying up the land, putting people out of the homes and property that had been in families for generations. If it was true, her blind trust in him and believing he was helping the

Cattleman's Association had been misplaced. Severely. Her hand trembled as she pushed the condiment dishes back into their proper place.

She went over and over the words in her head, positive of what she heard. The question was—what did she do with the information? Taking a deep breath to calm her nerves, she headed for the kitchen to wait for him to finish the call and figure out her next move.

She delivered an order to one of the customers sitting at the counter and topped off the man's iced tea, just as Mrs. Stanton approached the register. "Congratulations, dear. I just heard the wonderful news," the older woman said, reaching out to touch Becky's arm.

"Thank you." Becky ground out the reply, knowing there was nothing wonderful about the news anymore. The stares and questioning looks had been awful ever since the dance, but they would get worse before they got better when folks found out she'd broken the engagement off. But there was no way she could marry him and force herself to live with the traitor for a year. Luckily, Steve's duplicity, once exposed, would give the gossipmongers something else to talk about.

Mrs. Stanton paid her bill and left but not before sliding an extra twenty in Byron's fundraiser jar. Becky had meant to take it down this morning, but now she was glad she hadn't. By the looks of things, she would need every last penny.

Steve hung up the phone, a look of satisfaction on his face. Becky took a deep breath. She'd gone over and over in her head what to say, but now that the moment had come, she struggled with where to start. The last thing she wanted to do was tip him off that she knew the truth before she had time to talk to Jerry at the Cattleman's Association and warn him. Tipping her hand now would give him the chance to cover his tracks.

Becky slid in the booth across from him.

"What's wrong? Did you have a problem with a customer or a reporter?" Steve asked, obviously sensing her tension.

"Something like that." If one considered betrayal by the man she was about to marry a problem. Becky twisted her hands together in her lap, her nervous energy on overload.

"Okay. Want to talk about it?" he asked, frowning.

"No. Yes. Maybe." She glanced at the register, anything to avoid his gaze.

"Wow. I've never seen you quite like this. Maybe this will cheer you up. My mother released our wedding gift funds early. I wasn't sure how long after the wedding it would take, but now it doesn't matter."

She turned back to face him, surprised and pleased by the good news. At least until she remembered what she overheard. Their wedding gift was the dirty money he was going to use to buy up the McDougall property. The same money he planned to use to pay Byron's out-of-pocket medical expenses. Money that would destroy the people in town that she'd known all her life.

Not on my watch. She should have never agreed to marry him in the first place, and there was no way she was going to marry him now.

"I don't want to marry you anymore. The engagement's off," Becky said in a rush to get it over with. She pulled the engagement ring off and shoved it across the table. "This is yours. It was never really mine. I'm just the fool who was wearing it." Her voice broke on the last words. She was unprepared for the crush of disappointment in the region of her heart, the traitorous organ.

"What?" he said, his eyes wide with shock. "What's wrong? What happened?" He glanced down at the ring but didn't touch it. "Why are you doing this?"

"I've had second thoughts." *Second, third, and fourth, actually.*

"You had second thoughts in the last ten minutes?" He moved to take her hand, but she pulled back, staying just out of his reach.

"Yes," she said firmly, even knowing how silly she must seem to him. "I just don't want to do this anymore. Marriage is a special bond, something we don't share." And the last thing she needed was to be married to him when Steve's part in the ring of deceit was exposed. "I'll find another way to pay for Byron's surgery. Your poll ratings are higher than ever, and you don't need me anymore."

Steve ran his hands through his hair and shook his head, his jaw firmly clenched as he processed the news and her determination to end things. "I can't say I understand any of this, but I respect your decision. I don't want the ring. Keep it. Sell it. Whatever. I have no use for it." He slid the ring back across the table as she stood to leave. "And for your information, Byron's surgery is already scheduled—and paid for."

"What? Why would you do that?"

"Because I'm a man of my word. Once I learned I was getting the money, I called the hospital and transferred the deposit. I knew how important it was to you to get the surgery done as soon as possible. You did, after all, bring up my poll ratings, just as you mentioned." Steve's voice had taken on a crispness she didn't associate with him normally. If she didn't know any better, she'd think the breakup wasn't welcome news, and to a man who had adamantly not wanted marriage as a part of his life, his attitude made no sense.

She let out a huge sigh. It wasn't as if the money itself were dirty, just what Steve was using some of it for. It would be a mistake to let pride get in the way of her son's surgery. "Fine. I'll accept, given the circumstances, thank you. It's only fitting Parker money pay for it." They both knew exactly what she meant and it's what she wanted in the first place. She just hadn't known it would be Steve and not Jack, who would be part of the outcome.

"I will always do what's right for my nephew, regardless of what happens between us. And don't give me any sanctimonious bull crap. I want to spend time with him and not out of some sense of obligation. And at some point, we need to talk more about that particular situation. Becky, what's the real reason you're getting cold feet?" Why was he pressing her? They'd both gotten what they wanted.

"This discussion is closed." At least it was until she'd had a chance to talk to Jerry. She slid out of the booth and headed for the kitchen, determined not to let him see her cry. After work, she'd pay Jerry a visit. The head of the Cattleman's Association needed to know they were trusting the wrong man.

Chapter Seventeen

♥

JACK WAS WRONG. DEAD wrong. The final proof sparkled up at him. A gold digger would have never left the ring on the table. Whatever else was going on between him and Becky, Steve didn't have a clue, but one thing he did know was that it was time he had another chat with his brother.

Steve watched as she disappeared behind the kitchen door then turned to glance around the room, only to find everyone else's eyes on him. Becky had just jilted him, which a month ago would have been fine, but now, the breakup was met with a great sense of disappointment. He still couldn't believe it.

Just when he started to enjoy a different type of life, circumstances reminded him why it was a fool's notion. Love, marriage, and family life weren't for the likes of him. But why, then, did the sight of her walking away hurt so much?

There was no telling what would happen with the election still a month away, but he wouldn't chase after her and make a fool of himself. He should have known this wouldn't work out. Steve pocketed the ring, dropped a twenty on the table, and headed out the door. At least one person would be happy with the turn of events—his mother. And the gossipmongers would have a new tale to spin, one of romance and betrayal.

A week went by before Harry's initial fury over the breakup cooled, but Steve was still privately reeling.

Apparently, Becky dumping him made women feel sorry for him, and the ratings kept creeping up, not down. The phone rang off the hook, the women wanting to console him and be the next bride candidate. It was beginning to look like he'd win by a landslide, and he hadn't needed Becky after all. And he still had the money to help McDougall and the others.

He should be ecstatic, but instead, the feeling in the pit of his stomach could only be described as a feeling of loss. He missed Becky, and he missed Byron. More than he would have thought possible. They were the first bit of light he'd had in his life, and they'd become a bright light, one that, without knowing it, had been guiding him to consider that life held other possibilities than just a career.

The two happiest people with the turn of events were Harry and his mother. Harry, because of the rising ratings. His mother, thrilled to have won in the end. She never missed an opportunity to remind him of the million dollars he'd given up by putting her through a few extra days of turmoil.

"Tom London is on line four." Harry stood at the door to his office, looking a little flustered. "He's one of the more influential journalists, and we need to squash the rumor floating around. I think you should take his call."

"What rumor?" Steve had been buried in work, trying to catch up. A part of him was happy for the distraction because it kept him from thinking about Becky and Byron.

"That you broke it off with Becky and not the other way around. This won't play out well with our women voters, so I hope you can set him straight." The poor guy looked like he was about to have a hissy fit.

"It's no secret what happened—she clearly ended it. There were a lot of people at Charlie's who witnessed the whole thing." Steve shrugged. Things hadn't gone down the way he planned, and Becky's rejection still stung, so he honestly didn't care what the media said at this point.

"But they are saying you had a heated discussion and that she left crying. Crying, for Pete's sake. Somehow you managed to forget that detail when you told me the engagement was over. It's one thing when she was painted to be the bad person in the breakup, quite another if everyone starts thinking you did something to cause it and that you broke her heart. This isn't good. Not at all."

Some things were far more important than image. Becky was one of them, and in hindsight, he wished they'd been in a private location when she called it off. The media had been hard on her, and if there was a chance to get them to ease up, he'd take it.

"It was a mutual decision and not her fault. We broke it off, she gave the ring back, and then she left. It was common courtesy to let her do the walking away."

The reality was there hadn't been anything else he could do, the shock of her rejection still reeling in his brain and in his heart. He hadn't known about the tears. If he had, he might have fought harder for the truth. Crying meant emotion, as though she cared that it was over. Much the same way he did.

"Common courtesy?" Harry shot him a look of disbelief. "This was your fiancée. I thought you were in love with her. Fairy-tale love, an almost-at-first-sight romance. You haven't talked about it since you've been back, but I assumed that was because you were knee-deep in despair. I need the story because I've got to figure out damage control."

Poor Harry.

"There's nothing to tell beyond what you already know. You can tell that to Tom London. I'm running on my ability to handle the job and the successes of my career, not my personal life or marital status. Ramp up the ads, do whatever it takes to keep the ratings high, and squash the negative conversations. It's your job to spin this, so spin it." Steve was so over the demands of the election and the personal invasion of his life that came with it. Even though he'd expected it, nothing had prepared him for the reality.

"You don't have a personal life when you're running for office. You knew that before you asked her to marry you."

It was true. "I did and I do, but where anything concerns Becky, information is off-limits. If they want to know the color of my boxers, I'll be happy to share." Steve grinned, unable to keep from riling up Harry.

"I'm glad you think this is funny. If we lose because of your fickle behavior, you can count me off the team on your next run. I need people who thirst for the win." Harry turned and walked back to his desk.

He understood his manager's position, but lately, Steve found himself thinking more and more about other possibilities. Life outside the office. Becky had shown him what a happy life looked like, and the more he thought about it, the less he felt committed to the cause. And helping the McDougall family—now that felt great. There were lots of ways to serve the law, but not all of them came with the reward of friendship and a sense of doing right. *Fitting in.*

The Cattleman's Association now treated him as one of their own. Yes, he was a local, but even his father didn't fit in with that select group of men. They were upstanding, hardworking ranchers and farmers who understood the land and took pride in their family heritage. Something his father had never done.

Steve wondered how Becky had fared with all the media madness associated with their breakup. The more he thought about her, the more he remembered everything they did together, images of her laughing up at him never far away. The dance, the horseback riding, the park, game night at her house. And then back to the dance, a time when he'd held her in his arms protectively. Lovingly.

The times he'd spent with her were more like family than he'd ever experienced growing up. Several times, he'd reached for the phone to call her, but he always managed to convince himself it was better if he stayed away. He'd done enough damage.

But then Byron's surgery was Monday morning, and he intended to be there. What happened after that between them, he wasn't sure. He only knew he was looking forward to Monday morning. Whether Becky admitted it or not, Steve was family, and family stuck by each other.

That was with the exception of Jack and his father. His father, however, never reneged on his responsibility.

Steve picked up another file on his desk, the sticky note tagging it as a DBD. He opened it, but as he tried to read through the notes, all he could see was his brother's face. Letting him get away with this was wrong and not something Steve could allow.

He reached for the phone and dialed his brother.

"I heard you came to your senses and broke it off with the gold-digger." Jack's sinister laugh grated on his nerves.

"You heard wrong. She's not a gold-digger, and it was a mutual agreement." He wouldn't give Jack the satisfaction.

"Mother told me everything, so don't lie. Count yourself lucky is all I can say." Steve and Jack had never gotten along, but previously Steve managed to let his brother's lack of character go unchecked. That had been for his parents to correct, not that they did. Instead, they'd babied him, and it showed.

Steve counted to five before he continued. "Tell me about you and Becky. You said you were smart enough not to get caught. Was that before or after you found out she was pregnant with your child?" He moved in for the jugular, determined to throw his brother off course.

"That's a lie!" he shouted. "She's filling your head with lies and you believe them? That's rich coming from the guy who just dumped her." The derision in Jack's voice grated on his nerves.

"Why would she lie? It's not like she's after anything. In fact, she's never asked for anything from me, not one penny. Why is that, Jack?" The assumptive close had won many a case in the courtroom and Steve had no hesitation using it against his brother.

"Because I'm smart," Jack gloated. "She's a pushover."

"What's that supposed to mean?" He didn't want to hear anything about the time when his brother was with Becky, but if he was going to find a way to help her, he needed to dig up the dirt.

"I'm not admitting to anything." Which in itself was an admission of guilt. The trick was getting him to commit to a side.

It was time to push Jack harder and make a play for the truth. "There's such a thing as a paternity test."

"Stay out of it," Jack ground out.

"It's too late because I already know the truth. Byron is your son. Which makes him my nephew and part of our family."

"Believe what you want. You always were a sucker. I heard she's been spinning tales that I blackmailed her to keep quiet. She'll stoop to low-life levels to trap a guy. I already told you that."

This was news to Steve. News that made him grateful they were on the phone and not in the same room.

Otherwise, there was no telling what he would have done to his brother.

"Funny, this is the first I'm hearing about blackmail. Is that what you did, blackmail her?" He'd wondered about her silence, but now it all made sense.

"Why would I do that? The kid's not mine." But Steve heard a note of fear in his brother's voice now. He needed to press him harder before Jack had time to think.

Suddenly, it hit Steve like a streak of lighting. Becky's family was the only reason she would have agreed to anything with Jack, and her mother was the most logical person Jack would use for his sinister plan.

"It was her mother, wasn't it? Her mother worked for us." Now that their mother had fired Judith McAllister, the threat no longer existed. It explained why Becky felt comfortable enough to tell him in the first place.

"Nice try, but I'm still not admitting anything. You need to mind your own business," Jack threatened, sounding more like his father than he'd ever heard in the past.

"Then try this on for size. I'll get a court order that will force you to submit to a paternity test, and we'll let the entire ugly story play out for all the world to see. Mother and the Judge would love that. How long do you think they'll protect you when you sully the Parker name?" Steve played the ultimate ace in the hole, determined to verify the truth and then deal with it.

"You wouldn't. I'm your brother." Jack didn't sound so sure of himself now. He was used to playing with people's lives, but now he was the one doing the squirming.

"I would. The law is the law, and bringing deadbeat dads to justice has always been one of my personal mantras for this office."

"What do you want from me?" And there it was—Jack's admission of guilt. He had his brother right where he wanted him.

Time to put an end to his reign of terror over the McAllister family. "I want you to sign a parental release of rights and to pay back child support for the past five years into an account for Byron. I'll determine an acceptable amount, no arguments. I've already paid for his surgery, but I'm sure Becky can use the money for other related expenses."

"That's it? I get to walk away?" Jack was more than interested in the deal. It sickened Steve to realize his brother cared so little.

"Aren't you even the slightest bit interested in your son?"

"Nope. I never wanted kids." Jack's loss, because Byron was special, and the kid had the power to brighten someone's day.

"Do we have a deal?" Steve pressed harder, wanting closure.

"I expect complete confidentiality."

"That's fine. It's better for Becky and Byron anyway not to be associated with the likes of you."

"Why is that? She's a nobody," Jack huffed.

"So that people don't question her lack of judgment when she dated you. She really is a sweetheart."

"Clearly, you're blinded by love, but whatever. Draw up the paperwork and I'll have a check ready." Jack disconnected the call.

I've done it. Steve grinned.

An admission of truth, and better still, a parental release of rights. It was his gift to Becky for all she'd done for him. He couldn't wait to tell her, but first, he had to meet up with Jack and make sure he didn't back out of his end of the deal. He would also make sure Jack knew his parents would hear the truth. Anything beyond that would be between them.

Steve was more than pleased he managed to discover the truth without breaking his promise to Becky. The information, after all, had come completely from Jack.

Chapter Eighteen

♥

IT HAD BEEN A slow, painful week and a half. People stared, but most resisted the temptation to ask questions. Others weren't so discreet. A broken engagement was always big news in a small town. A few brave souls managed to get up the courage and ask but found themselves clueless when they walked away. Becky wasn't talking to anyone. Including the media.

It was great for the bottom line at Charlie's, and Ethan, the owner, had commented as much, all while making sure no out-of-towner journalists crossed any lines. A few of them managed to get pictures that were frequently splashed across the front pages of the tabloids, but in general, they had to get through Ethan, who'd become quite protective of her. Even the journalists camped out at her house became almost non-existent. Bottom line, Becky had nothing to say.

Other than to Jerry, and so far, she hadn't been able to talk to him, since he was out of town on business. Which meant Steve's duplicity had yet to make the news and take the spotlight off the breakup.

After Steve texted her the information on Byron's appointment last Friday, she hadn't heard from him again, which was just as well. It did no good to dwell on what was past or might have been. It had always been meant to be temporary—it just turned out shorter than expected. It didn't help that Byron was always talking about Steve and missing him. Or that her heart ached for him in the quiet of the night when there was far too much time to think about and remember the good parts.

Byron's first consultation appointment had gone well on Wednesday, as did the pre-op appointment on Friday. Monday was his surgery, and Becky was a bundle of nerves, something she worked extra hard on to keep Byron and the others from knowing.

Steve had some pretty major connections to make things move along as quickly as they were, and Becky was grateful for his help. And as nervous as she was about the surgery, she'd be relieved when it was over and they could go back to normal.

She drove to the school to pick up Byron, eager for her son's warm smiles. They held a special power that always seemed to make her feel better. And lately, she needed them a lot.

Knowing Steve was mixed up with the group trying to run people off their land, it made no sense that she missed him, but she did. Rumors were floating around about some big conglomerate trying to put together a mega-site for development. The idea of all the beautiful homesteads destroyed did nothing to help her mood.

Waiting outside the classroom door with the other parents, she scanned the children's faces as they poured out of the classroom when the bell rang. She spotted Byron at the front of the group.

"Hi, honey," she said, ruffling his hair when he came to stand next to her.

"Hi, Mom. We learned about elections today, and it made me think of Mr. Steve. Can we please go and visit him? I miss him." This wasn't the first time he'd brought up the subject. Her explanations of why he was gone went way over his head, and Byron had a determination streak in him a mile wide.

"I miss him, too, honey, but we're just friends now. And he's got a big job to do in Houston." It was true, and with the elections coming up, he would be swamped, even if she was considering stopping in to see him, which she wasn't.

"Look what I drew today." He held up a picture of the American flag.

"You did a great job. Wow." She smiled, taking the picture from him to keep it from getting crushed.

"It's for Steve. Maybe when we go see the doctor, we can stop and see him so I can give him the drawing." He looked up at her with big blue eyes that softened her response, even if she wasn't the intended recipient of his prized artwork.

She'd never had to compete with anyone for Byron's attention before, and she wasn't sure she liked it much. At least not now, after she knew the truth about him. "Maybe. I can't promise, though."

"Yeah! I'm going to see Mr. Steve! Maybe I'll draw him another picture before we go."

Becky let out a sigh. All Byron had heard was yes. Must be a kid thing. "That's a nice idea."

At home, Becky helped her mother clean up and get dinner ready. Her mother's severance check kept plenty of food on the table and the rent paid, but it wouldn't last forever. Maybe she could talk to Ethan about a job for her at the restaurant. Anything that would help the distance that had come between her and her mother over the whole sordid affair. She'd been okay with true love causing problems, but a two-week-later breakup after getting engaged, not so much.

After dinner, Becky sat out on the porch, a glass of tea in hand. She tightened her sweater against the evening chill as she looked up at the starry sky, remembering another time when she and Steve had sat in the exact same spot. He'd held her hand, the warmth comforting. *Safe.*

Thinking back over her life and the mistakes she'd made left her considering Steve's last comment about telling his family. Was she wrong in keeping Byron from his father's family, even if Jack didn't want anything to do with his son? Jack's threats no longer mattered. There was nothing he could do to her, so there was no reason to keep it a secret now.

Other than power and money. Steve assured her no one could take Byron away as long as she was a good mother, but what if he was wrong? What if the Parkers had people in high places who could circumvent the law? If they could offer two million dollars as a wedding gift, they could buy anyone off.

Friday morning, Becky arrived at work early, leaving her mother and sister to take care of Byron. She filled the condiment containers, rolled silverware napkins, swept the floor, and did everything else that needed to be done to make sure the place was ready to open at eleven.

The first customers straggled in a few minutes after the opening, and just like clockwork, lots of other townsfolk showed up. The regulars grabbed their favorite seats, and she went to work, hustling back and forth from the kitchen, trying to keep up with the orders and the newcomers. It was going to be a rough day with Katie calling in sick.

Becky dropped a check off at one table then started to clear the dishes from the next one over, into the gray plastic bin she used to haul the dirty dishes.

"Hey, Becky, can I get some coffee? I don't mind waiting for you to catch up before I order if I have some of that special brew to tide me over." Jerry grinned. The president of the Cattleman's Association was alone and just the person she wanted to talk to. There was no way she intended to let this opportunity pass to talk with him. No appointment needed.

"Sure thing." She picked up the pot of coffee and headed back to his table. "I've been needing to tell you something, but I've only got a few minutes." She lowered her voice, not wanting anyone else nearby to hear the conversation.

One eyebrow shot up as he gazed up at her, a questioning look in his eyes. "What's up?"

Becky sat in the chair across from him. It pained her to have to be the one to tell him, but it needed to be done. "You know the problems we've been having with foreclosures? Well, I think I know who's behind it. At least one of the guys. I figure you should know so you can be wary in your dealings with him."

"We have our suspicions, but who is this person you're referring to, and how did you come into your information?" He leaned forward, more than interested in her answer.

"Steve. Steve Parker." There. She'd outed him. And any backlash to his campaign was his own fault.

"No way. You've got it all wrong." Jerry sat back, a slight smile on his face.

He totally didn't believe her. She hadn't expected this.

"I overheard him talking when he was eating his lunch here not long ago." He had to believe her, or Steve would get away with his duplicity.

"Is this why you broke it off with him?" Jerry asked, a concerned look on his face.

Becky shrugged. "It's not like we were getting married for love." Jerry wasn't much for gossip, and she hoped he wouldn't repeat what she just said.

"I see." He leaned against the back of the booth, shaking his head. "This is bad."

"I know. So you believe me now?" Becky was relieved. She'd made the right choice telling Jerry.

"No. It's not that. Look, under the circumstances, I think you need to know the truth about Steve. It's confidential information, but I've never known you to be the gossipy type." It was no less than she thought of Jerry, but what was he talking about?

"What do you mean by the truth? Did you already know he was one of them?"

"No, Becky. He's one of us." Jerry spoke the words quietly, but they boomed in Becky's head.

One of us. It couldn't be.

"I know this has come as a shock, but if you two fought over this issue, you need to tell him you made a mistake and try to fix things. Anyone who's seen the two of you together can tell you're in love."

Jerry's warm and sincere smile touched her heart, but that was the only thing she was feeling. She didn't want to face what it meant if she'd been wrong.

"I can't believe it. Then what about the money?" She still didn't understand.

"We've set up a rescue fund to help landowners save their property by loaning them money to keep up with their payments during this recovery period from the drought." Jerry lowered his voice to barely above a whisper as he delivered another bomb. "Steve's our major contributor."

Becky gasped, shaking her head. *It isn't possible, is it?* She'd gotten it all wrong.

Steve's reason for needing the money was as altruistic as her own, and she'd severely misjudged his character. But it also meant the reasons she'd been fighting against her feelings for him didn't exist. Where did that leave her?

She knew exactly where. Broken-hearted. And the ache she felt was a hundred times stronger than when she'd been betrayed by Jack. She should have trusted her heart, but in the end, what she felt didn't matter.

Steve didn't reciprocate those feelings, and now that he didn't need the deal, he didn't need her.

"Thanks for telling me." Her whole body sagged in defeat.

Jerry laid his hand over hers. "Don't let him get away."

"It doesn't matter what I want—we live two separate lives. It was for the better, anyway." Steve had a life in Houston and Becky's was here. It would never work even if he did forgive her.

"But at least tell him how you feel. I thought women were good with all the mushy stuff."

She shrugged. "I'm not one of them." And she hadn't been since Jack.

Chapter Nineteen

♥

IT HAD TAKEN HIM the whole day, but Steve felt a level of satisfaction he hadn't felt in a long time. He glanced down at the manila envelope that contained everything he needed to finalize Jack's parental release. He hadn't minded meeting his brother halfway, preferring to get the ordeal over with.

After hours in a car, his muscles were stiff. He rolled his shoulders to loosen the tightness in his neck. His first stop was to see his mother, and with any luck, his father would have gotten his message and would join them. But it was the thought of seeing Becky again that gave him the extra push mentally *and* on the gas pedal as he headed back to Riverbend.

Becky would soon be done with her shift at Charlie's. He couldn't wait to share the good news and hoped to convince her to let him take Byron and her to the hospital tomorrow for the boy's surgery. Whether she wanted his help or not, he knew it was the right thing to do.

He pulled into his mother's driveway and was pleased to see his father's car parked in front. More than likely, out of curiosity since Steve had left the message firm yet vague.

The butler opened the door as he approached. "Good evening, sir."

"Good evening, Randall."

"They are waiting for you in the front room." The man's formal stiffness never sat well with Steve. He would have appreciated a doorman with a little personality, but then, maybe his mother controlled that the same way she did everything else. Well, he would soon tell her about something she couldn't control. What she did about it would be up to her.

"Thank you." Steve pushed open the door, entered, and spotted his parents on the far side of the room, each with a cocktail in hand. He made his way to where they stood. "Mother. Judge." He nodded, unable to keep the smirk from his face. He loved using his father's title because it irritated the old man, but also because Steve couldn't think of anything else to call him that he was comfortable with, except Thomas, and he would hate that even more.

"Well, this was certainly a surprise. I almost thought once I released your trust money, I wouldn't see you again." His mother was always direct, but tact wasn't her strong suit.

"Don't exaggerate. You know I'm busy at work. Besides, it's a two-way street to Houston last time I checked." He leaned forward to kiss her cheek out of habit.

"But there's so much to be done here. The Ladies' Society would be lost without my guidance." The woman had no small share of puff about herself.

"Can we all cut to the chase? I've got another meeting in thirty minutes," his father chimed in.

"Absolutely. You might both want to have a seat for what I need to say." His father's left eyebrow shot up, a surprised expression on his face. Wait till he heard the rest.

"I'm fine." His father tensed, a closed look on his face.

His mother took his advice and sat on the divan, sipping on her drink for fortification. "What is it, dear?"

"First, let me say this. What you are about to hear is confidential information. It can go no further than our family, not that you will want it to, but I've made a deal with the parties concerned." Steve wanted their promise and would accept nothing less.

"I don't like the sound of this already," the Judge bristled.

"And you won't, trust me. But I feel you have a right to know the truth."

"I promise, but I don't like it." His mother set her drink down on the table. "What is it we need to know?"

Steve looked up at the Judge and waited.

"Thomas, for heaven's sake, just agree. You have no choice."

"Fine. I agree." The Judge nodded, his mouth set in a tight line of disapproval. The man didn't like to be forced into anything.

"Byron McAllister is Jack's son."

His mother choked on her drink, and his father's clenched jaw and white-knuckled fingers as they gripped his glass were the tell-tale signs of how well they received the news.

"That's impossible. What's that little tramp been telling you?" His mother jumped to her feet, looking on the verge of an all-out fit.

"I think you should see this before you pass judgment. It takes two to make a baby, the last time I checked, but in this case, only one person took responsibility." He handed the documents to his father.

"What does it say, Thomas?"

"It's a release of parental rights. Signed by Jack." The Judge let out a deep sigh, one hand rubbing the back of his neck as he shook his head.

"She must have tried to trap him, and he knew about it. There has to be a reason." Her attitude rankled. Always protecting her baby boy.

"Whether you want to hear it or not, Jack is no saint. He was more concerned about his football career than he was about his own son. He blackmailed Becky into silence by threatening to have her mother fired and run out of town. Nice, huh?"

His father shook his head in disgust, his upper lip curled in a sneer. "Should have known the boy would disgrace us. Washed-up football player and living off his parents. I should have put an end to this a long time ago."

"I can't believe Jack would do this." His mother shook her head, still trying to comprehend the full extent of the news.

"Pull off the blinders, Mother. He's a love 'em and leave 'em kind of guy, and Becky was one of the first to fall for his sweet act. Heck, he's been fooling you for years—how do you think an eighteen-year-old girl would stand up to that? I know Becky, and I'd say her character is without question. It's Jack's that needs an overhaul." Steve leaned back against the piano and folded his arms. The questions would come, and he'd answer, but after a quick glance at his watch, he realized he didn't have long.

"So Byron is my grandson?" his mother asked, finally starting to process the information and what it meant to them personally.

"Yes, but you can't say or do anything about it." This was the tough part, which was why he'd extracted their promise first.

"I don't like anyone telling me what I can or can't do." The Judge's answer didn't surprise him.

"Doesn't matter. I gave my word to Jack and Becky not to reveal his identity. Therefore, you can't claim him. Not that you would."

"Why wouldn't I? He's my grandson. And based on you and Jack, he may be my only grandchild. The next generation. He needs to be raised like a Parker. Becky can't do that for him."

"That's where you're wrong. He's a McAllister. And unless Becky wants you involved, you must stay away. Don't get any bulldozing ideas, because this is one case I'd fight you to the end on." Steve leveled the Judge with a hard gaze, making sure he understood. This was no game.

"Then why tell us in the first place?" his mother asked.

"Because you had a right to know."

"And to think I let poor Judith go. I hated to do it, mind you. She was an excellent employee and knew exactly how I wanted everything. The new woman doesn't come close. How will I ever fix this?" His mother's anguish came across as genuine, surprising Steve. It was the first time he'd seen a compassionate side to her.

"You'll think of something, I'm sure." She always did.

"Thanks for telling us, son. I'll deal with Jack, don't worry." The Judge's tone didn't bode well for Jack, but that was between them. He'd done what he came here to do.

"That's between you three. Now, if you'll excuse me, I want to share the good news of the release with Becky. I'm driving them to the hospital in Houston tomorrow if she'll let me."

"Why wouldn't she let you?" His mother's gaze was suddenly confused, the idea of anyone refusing a Parker's helping hand inconceivable.

"Becky's not one of your society friends, Mother. She's a real person with real feelings and a big heart and a pure soul." She never wanted to be a part of the grand scheme playing out.

"You don't need to take that tone with me. Tell her I'm sorry. I understand why you were determined to help her and applaud your choices." His mother's sincere apology surprised him. It was as though she'd done a one-eighty, but he was still grappling with the change, unsure of where this was headed.

"We both had our reasons." Steve shook his head.

"I still don't know yours." The Judge's steely gaze zeroed in on Steve.

He shrugged. "To beat you. It's no secret." It didn't matter if his father knew the truth. The only thing that mattered was Becky and Byron.

"So why did you need the money?" he asked, persistent as always when he wanted information.

"Last time I checked, I'm an adult and don't answer to you anymore." If the Judge learned the truth about their fake marriage deal, there was no telling how he'd react, and Steve didn't want to know.

"See if you can talk to her, change her mind about keeping this a secret. I'm not against people knowing." It was as though the news she had a grandson had made her heart grow ten sizes.

The question was, could he trust her? Steve had promised Becky that Byron wouldn't be hurt by anything they'd done, and he meant to keep that promise. "That's a shocker. I'll talk to her, but I doubt I can change her mind. Her family's been hurt by the Parkers enough, and I'm not sure she's up to another round. Good night." Steve turned to leave.

He had a feeling Jack was only beginning to understand the repercussions of his actions. Five years overdue, but time.

The drive to Becky's was short, and before he knew it, he was knocking on the door.

Judith answered, her hands landing on her hips in a formidable gesture as she faced off with him. "If you're looking for Becky, she's not here."

"Good evening. I'm looking for her and Byron. I was hoping to take them to the hospital." At least she hadn't closed the door in his face.

Her expression softened, giving him hope she'd tell him where they were. He waited for her to make a decision, letting her come to her own conclusion about him.

"She took off from work early and left for Houston hours ago. They have an early appointment, so she wanted to stay there overnight and not do the drive in the morning to make it easier on Byron. And she wanted to treat him to dinner in the city."

A wave of disappointment washed over him, leaving an ache in the region of his heart. He was too late. "Oh, I'd hoped to drive them there myself. I need to talk to her. I guess I'll have to wait and see them at the hospital tomorrow."

"You're going?" Judith stepped through the door and closed it behind her, joining him on the porch.

"Of course I'm going. I promised Byron, and I want to be there to support Becky." He couldn't not go.

"You care for her, don't you? Aside from a hasty engagement and even hastier breakup," she added.

"I do...as a friend," he clarified. *More than a friend*, but he didn't think telling her mother that before he told Becky was a good idea.

"Cold feet happens to everyone. Just see that it doesn't turn your heart to ice." Her all-knowing look of wisdom settled on him like a lead weight.

"Good night." Steve turned and left, Judith's words echoing in his head.

Chapter Twenty

♥

BECKY GLANCED UP AT the clock but continued pacing the recovery room. The doctors had said forty-five minutes, and it was already five minutes past that window of time. "Thanks for coming to the hospital this morning, Kayla. I was a nervous wreck. *Correction*, am a nervous wreck. Byron, on the other hand, has been loving all the attention from the nurses." Becky gave a little half laugh. It was the most she could muster at this point. Her baby was in surgery, something no parent wanted for their child.

"He'll be fine. The hernia surgery is routine—and quit looking at the clock. I'm sure they'll be done any minute." Kayla crossed the room to grab her phone and send a text.

"I'm sure you're right. I still can't believe *you're* having a baby." It was a wonderful blessing neither she nor Dylan expected. Becky couldn't be any happier for her best friend.

"Me, either. The doctor didn't think it was possible. Shows how much they know." She grinned.

"Don't say that while Byron's in surgery. I want his doctor to know everything."

"You know what I mean."

She did, but fear kept her from viewing the comment lightly.

Kayla grinned. "You need to relax."

"I know. The voice of reason isn't very loud in my head at the moment."

"This pregnancy comes with one drawback—Dylan is adamant about me checking in with him throughout the day to make sure I'm okay and not overdoing it. To the point of overkill."

"He's a great guy, so enjoy it. Soon your attention will be claimed by a demanding and not very understanding infant. This is your time to be pampered."

The door opened, ending the conversation, and the surgeon came into the room.

"He did great," the surgeon announced, and Becky let out a sigh of relief. "Everything is back to normal. A couple of weeks of rest and he'll be good as new."

"Thank you so much, doctor. When can I see him?"

"They're just doing some last-minute checks on his vitals, and then they'll bring him here to monitor him until he's completely awake."

"I can't thank you enough. This is wonderful news." Becky was so happy she wanted to hug the doctor, but she wasn't sure of the protocol, so she just stood there awkwardly, smiling at him.

"If you have any questions, don't hesitate to ask," he said, clearly wrapping it up. "We'll keep him overnight for monitoring, but that's all routine. By morning, he'll be ready to go." The doctor made a few notes on his clipboard and turned to leave.

"Great. Thank you again."

The door closed behind him, and she turned to Kayla, grateful when her friend pulled her into a hug. The rush of emotion was overwhelming.

"I told you he'd be fine. Now relax, you don't want him to see you freaking out when he gets here." Kayla laughed.

Becky took a few deep breaths and said a prayer of thanks. Minutes later, the door opened, and a male nurse maneuvered Byron's bed through the door. He looked peacefully asleep.

"Is he okay?" she asked.

"He's doing fine. Just give him a few more minutes," the nurse reassured her.

She watched as the man changed out the cables that hooked Byron up to the room monitors. Becky's eyes never left the screen once the beeps and lines started registering all sorts of information.

"Thank you for taking such good care of him."

"No problem. He's been a little charmer, according to the other nurses." The man smiled as he tucked the blanket up around Byron more tightly.

Byron's eye's fluttered open. "Mommy," he squeaked out.

"Yes, baby. Mommy's right here." She held his hand. "And Aunt Kayla's here, too."

Kayla stepped up to the bed. "Hey, kiddo. Heard you were a real trooper, and now you're good as new." She ruffled the top of his head.

Byron smiled. "Hi, Auntie Kayla. I didn't know you were coming to see me." His voice was getting stronger.

"Of course, I came. You're my favorite little man."

Byron drifted back to sleep.

"It's okay. He'll keep doing that for a while. The anesthesia is wearing off and the pain meds will kick in," the nurse explained. "I'll be back in to keep checking on him and we have a nurse watching the monitors in case we're needed."

"Thanks for letting me know." The nurse left, the door swinging shut behind him.

Becky sat on the edge of the bed, watching her son sleep. *My little angel.*

The door opened again, and someone entered. Becky twisted around, surprised to find Steve standing there, a stuffed teddy bear tucked under one arm and a large envelope in his hand.

"Hey there. How's he doing?" Steve entered the room and crossed to the bed, placing his hand on her shoulder, offering comfort.

Becky was torn, her reaction to his presence both good and bad. Her heart skipped a beat, but then she remembered they weren't together and there was nothing between them. And now wasn't the time to focus on her feelings. "He's doing great. He just got out of surgery, and he's sleeping."

"Wonderful news. Good to see you again, Kayla. I was glad to hear you'd be with Becky throughout this, knowing she'd need all the extra support she could get."

"It's nice to see you, too." Kayla shot him a smile and then looked back at her.

Becky tried to wrap her head around the fact Steve had shown up today. "Wh...what are you doing here? And how did you get past the nurse's station?"

"Well, about that..." He grinned. "I sort of told them I was your fiancé, and since they recognized me as a candidate for the D.A.'s office and our relationship is public knowledge, they sort of bent the rules for me."

"Sort of? They must have missed the breakup part of the media hype. You always were a sweet talker and could get just about anything you wanted." She shook her head, knowing she was one of those women he could sweet talk. Her heart ached for him each and every day, but it was over. And it was time her heart started agreeing with her brain. All of Steve Parker's reasons for wanting to marry her no longer existed.

"Why don't I head downstairs to the cafeteria and grab something to eat?" Kayla picked up her purse and headed for the door.

"You can stay." Becky frowned, sending her friend a silent message.

"No, I'm good. I really need food." And just like that, she was gone, leaving her and Steve alone. She couldn't have been any more obvious.

Becky turned to Steve. "It's sweet of you to come, but why are you here?" she asked.

"I promised Byron I would, and to offer you support. I would have been here earlier, but traffic was backed up on the interstate because of an accident. I got here as soon as I could."

"But that promise was before...you know...the breakup."

"A promise is a promise in my books." Steve smiled. "But since we're alone and he's asleep"—he nodded toward Byron—"I need to tell you something. I've got some great news for you." Steve had an air of excitement about him that echoed his words, his upbeat meter overflowing, looking handsome as ever. Her heart did a somersault just being in the same room with him.

"What is it?"

"It's about Jack."

Becky went into alert mode, not liking the subject matter one bit. "What about him?"

Steve set the bear on the bed for Byron and handed her the manila envelope he'd been carrying. "See for yourself."

She pulled out the pages and glanced at them. Legal docs of some sort. Becky read the first couple of lines. "I don't understand. How—" She got off the bed and moved toward the window, motioning for him to follow her across the room. Becky wanted to be out of earshot in case Byron woke up again.

"Jack's release of parental rights. Byron is all yours. And the how doesn't matter." Steve grinned as if he'd just given her the greatest gift ever. *Which it was.*

"It does matter. I love this, and it's the best news ever, but this means you went to Jack. You promised you'd stay out of it. What happened to a promise is a promise?" She shook her head as she began to consider the repercussions of his news.

"I didn't tell him anything you said to me. But the law is the law, and he needed to take responsibility for his actions, one way or the other. I confronted him with information I'd already guessed before you confirmed things, and he buckled under the pressure, admitting everything. So, you see, the information came from him. And it was my job to handle the details."

It was hard to believe Jack would just walk away completely, but now, her fear of him coming back into their lives was over. Jack was powerless. "What about your parents? Do they know? What stops them from trying to claim grandparent rights?"

"Also covered. Jack made me promise confidentiality going forward, but I was clear the grandparents weren't part of the agreement. They deserved the truth. I talked to them yesterday but warned them to stay away from you and Byron unless you direct otherwise. You are in complete control. I wanted you in on any decisions made that would affect his future."

He didn't understand. Couldn't understand what it was like to have the threat of someone taking your child away hanging over your head.

"And how'd they take that? They can squash someone like me." She shook her head, her agitation growing as she struggled to comprehend the magnitude of what Steve had done.

"Someone like you? You're strong, beautiful, confident, and one heck of a mama bear when it comes to her cub. They don't stand a chance. Besides, I have their promise. In fact, it's rather funny."

She didn't see an ounce of humor in the situation. "How so?"

"We both know the very idea would have been upsetting to them, but then the idea of being told they couldn't have something made them want it more. I'm sure they will be more than accommodating to you and your family going forward. After all, you hold the keys to what they seem to think will be their only grandson." He laughed.

This was something she would have never foreseen. Steve must be one heck of an attorney to not only elicit a promise from his parents, but then completely turn the tables. "Okay, sounds reasonable." She let out a deep breath. "It's a lot to take in, and I need to think about what this could mean, with or without them in Byron's life. I've lived for so long without anyone knowing, it's hard to suddenly have that change."

"I understand. There's one other thing. I wouldn't have been doing my duty if I didn't get this at the same time." He handed her a check.

Her eyes widened as she noticed the amount...and it was written out to her. Signed by Jack. "Is this—"

"Child support. For the five years he was responsible for Byron before giving up his rights."

"That's a lot of money." She couldn't help the rush of excitement that sizzled through every pore of her body. This money could change everything. It would allow her the chance to do more for Byron, her mother, and her sister. It was a godsend.

"He doesn't have a job, but I proposed a number I felt fair, and he was willing to accept my terms with the confidentiality clause."

Becky had never been after money, with the exception of Byron's surgery, but this...this was incredible. The real problem, however, was Steve.

He was doing his job. This was all about the law and nothing to do with her. She'd fallen in love with a man who saw life through dollar signs. Because there was no doubt in her mind that's what had happened, because the ache she felt in the region of her heart could only be one thing. It was a good thing he didn't know the truth.

"Thank you. It'll come in handy." She stepped closer to give him a hug, his arms coming around her automatically. It felt good to be back in his arms, and for a brief second, she wished she could stay there.

Someone came through the door and coughed. She turned to find her mother watching them with interest.

"Mom, I didn't know you were coming."

"Of course I would. Byron is my grandson. How is he?" She nodded toward the bed, crossing the room to stand by the bedside.

"He's doing great. Sleeping but the doctor said he'll go in and out a few times before he stays awake for any extended period."

"Wonderful. It's nice to see you here, Steve." Her mother winked at him.

"Thanks. I should probably get going. I need to stop by the courthouse this afternoon and file this." He held up the envelope. "Tell Byron I stopped in to check on him and that I'll be back later."

"Okay, and Steve, thanks." Becky smiled. His generosity only ramped up the guilt she felt for not trusting him. She had to tell him the truth, but not now. Today was about Byron and not her mistakes.

"Anytime." He dropped a kiss on Byron's head.

"I wasn't trying to run you off," her mother said, her gaze going back and forth between them.

"You're not. Have a nice day, ladies." And then he was gone.

The sight of Steve kissing Byron's forehead and the compassion in his eyes left her raw with emotion. Steve was caring and loving, and more like a father than Jack had ever been. He was a man she would be proud for her son to be just like.

"I don't know what's going on between you two, but that sure didn't look like a broken-up couple to me when I came through the door. Want to talk about it?"

"No. Yes. There's something you should know, something I should have told you a long time ago. Jack Parker is Byron's father." It was easier just to say it and get it over with. She waited for the disappointment on her mother's face, but it didn't come.

"Honey, I was pretty sure it was him all along."

"But you never said anything." Becky gazed up at her in confusion.

"Didn't have to. I'm your mother. Besides, the little JP in hearts written all over your notebooks was a giveaway. Especially when not long after that, they were blacked out with a marker and then you turned up pregnant. Honey, mistakes are made even when we have the best of intentions not to. My love for you has never been conditional. I figured if you wanted to tell me, you would." Her mother's soft smile was full of understanding.

"I couldn't. His identity will remain confidential, but I want you to know why I couldn't. I'm tired of running and hiding the truth. He blackmailed me into silence." Becky's vision blurred, her eyes glazing over with tears. It was over. The whole ordeal was over if Steve was to be believed.

"What? Oh, honey, you *should* have come to me. What a despicable thing to do." Her mother stiffened, her brow drawn tight in anger. It was easy to see where Becky got her protectiveness of Byron.

"I couldn't. He threatened to have his parents take Byron. And he was using you. Your job. He threatened to have you fired for theft and run out of town. He can't do that now, though, can he?" She smiled, realizing it was true.

Not to mention the paper she held in her hand, courtesy of Steve. She didn't like him taking matters into his own hands without her permission, but she also understood it was his job to uphold the law. It was hard to stay mad at the man.

"No, they can't do a thing to me. There must be something we can do to stop the jerk. He shouldn't be able to get away with this."

"Steve just did." She held up the papers. "Parental release forms. Jack gave up all rights to Byron and can't touch him now. And get this, back child support for the five years he was responsible." She handed the check to her mother.

Her shocked expression mirrored Becky's own when she'd seen it. Fifty thousand dollars was a lot of money.

"That's wonderful. And so is Steve. I've seen the two of you together. He cares about you. I think you should give him another chance."

"He's not asking for one." Becky wanted him to, but she also knew how important the election and his career were to him.

"Don't make another mistake and let the man get away," her mother insisted.

"He's a friend. I know you won't like what I'm about to tell you, but the engagement was an arranged deal.

He paid for Byron's surgery, and in return, Steve got the poll ratings from having a family and appearing settled. Not to mention, he got a very sizable wedding present out of this. We both got what we needed, and that's all it ever was. Although, at the time, I didn't realize he was helping the Cattleman's Association."

"I hate that you felt the need to lie about it. Although at times I wondered at the haste. But I also saw the way he looks at you and Byron when he thinks no one is watching. Make no mistake, he cares. A lot. Some men need a little help to figure out what's important in life."

"He's a Parker, and we live in two different worlds. His life is in the city, and mine is in Riverbend." Becky crossed the room to stand by Byron, picking up his hand, needing the connection.

"Him being a Parker should have nothing to do with it. He's not Jack Parker, and that's what matters. Those two brothers are as different as night and day. But it is nice to hear you call Riverbend your home. I've always known you wanted to leave and that when Byron came along, it smashed all your dreams."

"Sometimes dreams change for the better." Becky thought of the empty store on Main Street and sighed. She'd pictured it a hundred times before, all laid out perfectly as her own coffee shop. Someday maybe. Although the check for fifty grand she'd received would go a long way to making it a reality.

The nurse walked in, and all discussion ended. "I'm here to check his vitals."

"Becky, why don't you take a break and get something to eat or go outside for some fresh air? I'll stay with Byron."

"Thanks, Mom. That sounds like a plan. And by the way, what I told you has to remain a secret between us."

"That's fine, dear. Just think about what I said, though."

Becky hurried out of the room, eager to find Kayla. She didn't have a clue what to do about anything, part of which included the Parker parentals. They were, after all, Byron's grandparents.

Chapter Twenty-One

♥

STEVE WAS SORRY NOT to catch Byron when he was awake, but the trip to the courthouse and the call he'd scheduled on his way to Houston wouldn't wait. He'd go back after, but duty called. Becky had said everything went well, the sense of relief overwhelming. In a short amount of time, the kid had crept into his heart. *My nephew*. It had a nice ring to it.

Back in his office, he closed the door, not wanting anyone to hear his call with Jerry. It was enough his father's parting comment left him wondering just how much the Judge knew, but clearly, it wasn't enough to call him out for anything. But when he learned the truth about what Steve was up to, Judge Parker would have plenty to say and none of it good. And it would come out sooner or later. He wasn't naive about small-town gossip channels.

Steve had firmly pitted himself on the opposite team and was willing to put an end to any shenanigans from the Judge's wealthy cronies trying to get wealthier. His phone rang, and Jerry's name popped up on the screen.

"Hey, there. What did you find out?" Steve asked, getting straight to the point. They weren't scheduled for another meeting for a week, so this had to be important. He hoped the bank wasn't making another move so soon.

"That's one of the things I like about you—straight and to the point. The Cattleman's Association called a special meeting last night, and we have a proposal for you."

"I'm listening." Steve glanced out the window of his office, watching the usual flurry of activity.

"You know the issues we have going on with the local bank, but we aren't the only place this is happening. I'm getting more calls and it seems whoever's doing this is getting more aggressive and starting to spread their borders outside Tumble County."

"I'm looking into it, and you know I'm doing the best I can, but I can't promise funding for the entire state. We agreed to limit it to the county, at least until more funds were resourced to help out the interim loans."

"I know, and that agreement stands. It's also why the Association wants to put you on a retainer to work for us full-time. You could set up an office here, keep your finger on the pulse better, and learn more. I know all about the election, and I realize this is poor timing, but we wanted you to know all your options before you went through with the election. There are several people who can take your place on the D.A.'s platform, but none who can do what you're willing to do to help those in need of legal assistance. Think of how much more you could do for the people of Texas than sitting behind the cloak of the D.A.'s office." Jerry dropped the bomb without hesitation, using more than a little persuasion in his tone.

But give up on the election? *The idea is ludicrous.* "I couldn't possibly walk away now. I mean, it sounds like a great opportunity to go out on my own, and the Association would be a huge client to get started, but that's not my goal. My goal is the judge's seat, and that requires me to put in my time as D.A."

"I told them you'd say that, but I also told them I'd present the idea. Speaking of the judge, how is your father?"

"Crafty and miserable as always." It might be his father he was talking about, but that didn't stop Steve from speaking the truth.

"And that's what you want for your life?" The comment struck home.

"Touché. Well played, Jerry."

"Just promise me you'll think about it. It's not too late." They talked a few more minutes about what was happening and then ended the call. Steve rubbed his head with the palm of his hand, trying to clear his brain.

Why would anyone even propose such an idea? Leave the election race? *No way. Have a life?* He couldn't do it. He'd spent too much time getting here, and he couldn't possibly walk away. Not to mention, Harry would kill him.

Steve sat back in his leather chair and gazed out the window. The election was two and a half weeks away. The decision was out of his hands. He glanced at his watch and left the office, determined to get back to the hospital to visit Byron.

And Becky, if he was honest.

After checking in with the nurse at the front desk of Byron's floor, he made his way down the hall to the kid's room. Byron was talking a mile a minute as he walked in, but the kid's expression lit up like the Fourth of July when he saw who was here to visit. Steve's heart grew another size bigger.

"Mr. Steve, you came." Byron's sweet smile was a joy to behold. The kid had been through a lot but kept a positive and bright attitude.

"Yes, just like I promised." He crossed the room to ruffle the boy's hair.

"Thank you for my bear. I love him. I'm going to call him Ferris."

Steve grinned. "You're welcome, kiddo. And I love his name. How are you feeling?"

"I'm good as new, and Mommy says I'm going home in the morning."

Steve looked over at Becky and her mother and smiled. "Hello, ladies. If you want a break, I'll sit with Byron. I can read him a story if you brought any books."

"Oh, we brought books, but he doesn't stop talking long enough to listen to one." Becky laughed.

"Hey, it's not every day you have hernia surgery. You were very brave, Byron."

The kid beamed under his praise. "Thanks, Mr. Steve. You can go get something to eat, Mommy and Grandma. Let us guys stay and read. I promise I'll be good."

"Stuck in bed, it's not like you have much choice, but fine, I'll leave you two alone for a bit." Becky stood and headed for the door. "Coming, Mother?"

"In a bit. Why don't you go downstairs? I'll join you in a minute." A strange look passed between the two women.

"What are you up to now?" Becky asked, holding the door open.

"Nothing. I just want to talk to Steve for a second." Judith wasn't backing down, and it fanned his curiosity.

"Then why don't you two step outside the room to chat, and then you and I can both go downstairs together? Byron doesn't need to hear grown-up talk." Becky came back into the room.

"Fine by me." Judith headed for the door, expecting him to follow.

"But you're not leaving, right, Mr. Steve?" Byron asked before Steve made it to the door.

"I'm not leaving. I'll be right back, I promise." Steve nodded.

"And a promise is a promise. Just like the one you told me before. I like promises." Byron settled back against his pillow, satisfied he wasn't leaving.

"I do, too, buddy." Steve shot him a wink before following Judith into the hall. "What's going on?"

"I just wanted you to know Becky told me everything. And I mean everything." Her meaning was clear. It was a huge start knowing Becky was making things right and moving forward.

"That's great. Does it change anything between you and me?"

"Not at all. You're not responsible for your brother. I wanted to say thank you for all you've done for Byron and Becky." Her mother stepped forward and gave him a hug.

"You're welcome. It was my pleasure, honestly." He nodded.

"I don't mean to meddle, but I see what I see. You may not admit it to me, but a mother knows when someone cares more for her daughter than as just a friend. And Becky cares about you. A lot. She's not good at showing it. Ever since your brother did her wrong, she hasn't trusted people. Give her time to come around. Don't walk away from what anyone who sees you two together recognizes."

"And what's that?"

"That you love her." *Love*. Not a word he'd ever applied to anyone before.

The trouble was he didn't want to walk away, but what choice did he have? She'd already told him flat out she wouldn't leave Riverbend, and nothing else had changed.

The two women left to go downstairs, giving Steve and Byron time to hang out. Byron doted on his every word, especially when Steve played charades with the teddy bear. It was child's play, but it turned out to feel immensely rewarding.

If he had a son, he'd want him to be exactly like Byron. Except there was no room in his life for kids.

Unless you change things. And it was his life to change.

Becky returned, her mother staying downstairs to make a call.

Steve's pulse raced when she entered the room. Becky looked refreshed from her time away. "Did you manage to relax?"

"Hi, Mom," Byron called out.

"I did, and hi to you, too, kiddo. Have fun?" Becky crossed the room to Byron's bedside and dropped a kiss on his forehead.

"Yes, we played Goldilocks and the Three Bears." Byron's smile warmed his heart.

"That's something I would have liked to see." Becky's sweet laugh warmed his heart more.

"Show her, Mr. Steve. Do the baby bear first," Byron pleaded.

Steve looked at Becky for help. It was one thing to do it for Byron, quite another to make a fool of himself in front of Becky.

"Come on, Steve. Give it a go. I can't wait to hear this." Laughter twinkled in her eyes as she made the request. She knew darn well it would be humiliating.

"As long as this never leaves this room. My reputation would be shattered." He couldn't believe he was letting her talk him into this.

"Fine. I won't record it and post it all over the internet. How's that for a promise?" Becky laughed more, her eyes watering.

"And a promise is a promise," Byron chimed in, smiling.

He was too darn smart and cute for his own good.

"This bed's too hard. This bed's too soft. This bed's just right," Steve squeaked out the words in a high, girly voice, his embarrassment complete.

Becky laughed out loud, while Byron went into a fit of giggles all over again. "That's adorable."

"Do Papa Bear. You got to hear this, Mom."

Steve resigned himself to the task of amusing the two of them. "Who's been sleeping in my bed?" he said, his voice low and gruff. Another fit of laughter and he was done. "That's it, I've got to go."

"Aww, shucks. I like it when you're here. I've missed you, Mr. Steve."

"I miss you, too, kiddo. Maybe I can work something out with your mother, and we can all get together and do something fun." Steve looked up at Becky, hoping she'd say yes, realizing how much her answer meant to him.

"I'd like that." Her soft, sweet smile reassured him she meant every word.

"Great, then it's a date. I'll get in touch with you when I have something planned." He hadn't felt this excited since their last outing. "Do you need any help tomorrow getting Byron home?"

"No, but thanks. Mom is staying the night and following us home."

"Perfect. Just let me know if you need anything." Steve reached for her hand, loving the feel of it in his. It felt right.

"Okay, and Steve, I mean it, thanks for everything." Her smile melted any remaining cold spots in his heart.

He stepped forward to hug her, glancing over at Byron who sat there watching them, a huge smile on his face. And it was in that second, he knew the truth. He did love her. And he loved Byron.

Everything he wanted was right here in this room. This was what made him happy. Not the job. Not beating out his dad. He could still be an advocate for the underserved with a position in Riverbend. He wanted his personal life back, his priorities straight, and a chance at happiness with the woman in his arms.

He knew the attraction between them hadn't faded. If anything, it was stronger. Becky was different than anyone he'd ever met, and she wasn't anything like his mother. She was warm, sweet, caring. And he wasn't anything like his father and didn't want to be. His goals were all wrong, and he was missing out on his chance for a real life.

A life he wanted with Becky.

By the time he left the hospital parking lot, he knew exactly what he needed to do, and Harry was the first stop on his long list of to-dos. He dialed his campaign manager's number.

"What's up?" Harry answered.

"We need to talk. Can you meet me at Patron's in an hour?" The sooner they had the talk, the better.

"What's this about? Should I be worried?" Harry's voice was tense. Unfortunately, things would get worse for him before they got better.

"We'll talk at Patron's."

"Fine. See you there." Harry's voice came out sharp. Unsettled. The man was good at his job and sharp as a tack, so it wouldn't surprise Steve if he was already guessing the purpose of the meeting. Harry, the campaign manager wouldn't like the decision one bit, but Harry, his friend, would get over it.

Chapter Twenty-Two

♥

BYRON WAS BACK TO normal within the two weeks the doctor had predicted. Becky was relieved it was all behind her, all except the part that included Steve. Her mother sang his praises all the time and Becky was tired of hearing them.

Not that she didn't agree, but he'd failed on his promise to Byron, leaving her to explain his continued absence to her son. He got a pass on a technicality when he told his parents about Byron, but it didn't excuse making a promise to a little boy he didn't intend to keep.

Not to mention, his absence had also kept her from telling the truth about her false assumption, something she desperately needed to do for her own peace of mind.

She still couldn't believe he'd walked away from the campaign and passed the torch to Tim Stutts, the man who ended up winning the election. But, if anything, it should have freed up more of his time, making it worse that he hadn't shown up.

Becky waved to an older couple as they got up to leave after lunch. "Have a nice day," she called out to them. She pocketed the tip and cleared the table, returning to wipe it down and rearrange the condiments and napkins to where they belonged. The bell over the door jingled just as she headed through the back kitchen door carrying the bin of dirty dishes.

She was tired and, for once, hoped the newcomers wouldn't sit in her section. Walking through the swinging door, she glanced around and then let out a sigh of relief, her section still empty.

"Becky," an all-too-familiar voice called to her from by the register. *Steve.*

Her pulse raced—not that she wanted it to. She cared far too much about him, but it could only spell heartache for her. Kayla and her mother were wrong. Steve Parker was not the man for her, not by a long shot.

"What brings you here?" She tried to keep her voice as casual as possible.

"You. Byron. We need to talk." Steve looked completely at ease, his gaze never leaving her face.

"It's been two weeks, and I haven't heard a word from you. Nothing. Byron asks about you every day. I figure the time for talking is over." The resentment she'd been feeling slipped out.

"I couldn't agree more." *What?* She hadn't expected him to agree with her.

"Then there's nothing left to say between us," she huffed.

"I think I've always been a talker—it comes as an attorney privilege. I decided two weeks ago you needed more than words—you needed action. I didn't want you to hear pretty words and have them fall on deaf ears."

"What are you talking about? And why didn't you follow through on your promise?" She was more confused, his ability to redirect conversation, losing her completely.

"I'm talking about us. And I did follow through on my promise. I'm here, aren't I? I didn't specify when, and I had things to do before I could visit the two of you." Steve's smile melted her resistance, but not enough to thaw her heart.

"Fancy lawyer talk."

"I've been super busy, but if it means anything, I've missed you." He sounded so sincere. And the twinkle in his eyes was a reminder of how he'd looked during the times he'd kissed her.

She shoved the memory aside. She wanted to believe him, and she'd missed him, too, but she needed to protect her heart. She loved this man, and because of that, he had the power to hurt her more than Jack had ever done. "Byron's missed you, too. Why did you pull out of the election? I thought that was your dream."

It had been big news, and everyone in town talked of nothing else for days. At first, she hoped he would call and that maybe she'd had something to do with his change of heart. But as the days passed and there'd been no word from him, she knew better than to hold out hope.

"Like I said, I'd rather not *explain.*" Steve stepped in closer, bringing them face-to-face.

"I understand." Totally untrue, but it was hard to think with him standing this close.

"I doubt it." He grinned. "Please come outside and give me five minutes of your time. I want to show you something. Then you'll understand. I promise." He pulled her toward the door, but she resisted.

"You and your promises—"

"Have always been golden and always will be."

Something in his smile melted every ounce of resistance, and she gave in. "Fine. Five minutes." She spotted Ethan at the bar. "I'm going on a break. I'll be right back."

"Sure thing. Take your time. I'll make sure if anyone sits in your section that they're taken care of."

Curious stares followed her and Steve as he led her out the front door of the restaurant. "What's going on?"

"Trust me on this." He grinned, looking like he owned the world.

He took her by the arm and led her down the sidewalk. They'd gone two blocks before he came to a halt, stopping in front of the store on the corner.

She'd heard the place recently sold. It looked different, the for-sale signs gone and the boards removed. Brown paper covered the windows. The new owner must want privacy while they redesigned the place. "What are we doing here?"

"This." Steve walked up to the window of the store and pulled on the brown paper.

"What are you doing? You're going to get arrested if you're not careful." Becky glanced up and down the street to reassure herself the sheriff was nowhere in sight.

He laughed. Not exactly the response she expected.

"Look," he said, pointing to the writing on the front of the window.

Coffee Corner.

It wasn't possible. "Is this..." She didn't know how to ask, didn't dare dream.

"It's yours." Steve moved to stand next to her, taking her hand in his and drawing her closer.

"How did you know about the name? I never mentioned that to you."

"Your mother." Steve stood there grinning.

"She knows about this place?" Becky was flabbergasted.

"Some." He winked.

"I can't believe you would do this. You should have asked me first. I can't afford this. I know I got the money from Jack, but I prefer not to touch it unless it's for Byron." The cost of the place had to far exceed what she could ever afford. And then there was the upkeep and supplies and staff. It would take more money than she had to make a go of the place.

"I like that about you. In fact, there's a lot about you I like. But it's not for sale, so you can't buy it." Steve moved to stand next to her and drew her in his arms.

"I don't understand why you would do this. It's too much."

He took her by the hand and started walking. "Follow me."

They crossed the street, where Steve stopped in front of the old apothecary. It had been closed for over ten years, but now the place had brown paper across the windows.

Familiar brown paper. It was like déjà vu as Steve walked up to the window and yanked the paper off to reveal the new name of the place.

Steve Parker, Attorney at Law.

Becky looked up at him, trying to wrap her brain around what she was seeing.

"I told you showing works better with you, and judging by the expression on your face, it worked." Steve took her hand and raised it to his lips.

"You're moving here? Leaving the city?"

"I am. And the Cattleman's Association is my first client, which should keep me quite busy."

"Yeah, about that, it would have been nice if you'd share the little tidbit with me about you working with them." Becky nodded. It was time to come clean with Steve, and she hoped he would forgive her lack of trust.

"It wasn't exactly public knowledge," he said, pulling her close.

"Still, Jerry had to tell me the truth after I accused you of being in cahoots with the bad guys."

Jack had tainted her ability to believe in the goodness of people, but Steve had restored her faith.

"That's rich." Steve chuckled, shaking his head.

"I'm so sorry I didn't believe in you. Can you ever forgive me?"

"Consider it done. You asked me why I withdrew from the election? It's because you and Byron are more important than winning the judge's seat. I wanted to be near you."

Tears ran down her face. He'd done this for her and Byron. And he'd forgiven her. But it didn't change anything when it came to the Coffee Corner. "I like the sound of that a lot. But I can't accept this." She pointed to the Coffee Corner, although it pained her to turn down her dream. "It's too much."

"Not if it's a wedding present. I love you." Steve reached into his pocket and withdrew something, dropping to one knee and then taking her hand.

Somewhere in the far recesses of her brain, she registered what he was doing, but most of her brain was still stuck on the words "*I love you.*"

"Rebecca McAllister, will you marry me? For real this time." He looked up at her with love shining in his warm brown eyes that twinkled. *For real.* Magical words that filled her with a rush of emotion knowing he felt the same way she did.

Dreams did come true, and there really was a happily ever after meant for her.

"I love you, too," she said through her tears. "And yes, I'll marry you. For real this time." Her heart burst with joy. *Steve loves me.*

He stood and pulled her into his arms as clapping and cheers surrounded them.

Becky looked around to discover several people from town had gathered around, including her mother. It seemed a lot of people knew what had been happening, but lost in her own misery, she'd missed the clues.

"You really do love me?"

"I really do." Steve lowered his head to kiss her. It was like coming home.

Two arms wrapped around her mid-section. She looked down to find Byron hugging them both tight. Steve swung her son up in his arms.

"Hey, little man. Thanks for giving me permission to marry your mother." Steve grinned, giving Byron a high five.

"You knew, you little stinker." Becky ruffled Byron's hair and kissed his cheek.

"Yup. I'm good at keeping happy secrets." Byron laughed, his arms tightly wound around Steve's neck.

"You sure are. The best." Her son beamed under Steve's praise. Correction, soon to be *their* son. It had a nice ring to it.

Epilogue

Steve picked Byron up, putting him on his shoulders, and carried him toward the swing set, setting him down in the sandbox to play. Becky joined them seconds later. He loved watching his wife walk into a room, lighting it up and bringing joy to those around her. Today, the glow was brighter than ever, and with good reason on multiple accounts.

He couldn't believe how incredibly blessed he was to have her and Byron in his life. Although he hadn't given her long to put together the wedding, she'd managed to make it memorable—a church wedding, followed by a reception in the gardens at his parents' house. It had been the perfect backdrop for her beauty. And after the honeymoon, they'd had the grand opening for the Coffee Corner, and it was a huge success, mostly because of Becky's determination.

"How are you feeling, sweetheart?"

"I'm good, thanks to you." Becky grinned, hooking her arm around his.

They'd come a long way in a short time, and he wouldn't change a thing.

Steve still couldn't believe Becky and his parents had become friends, but then, Becky had a way of working her magic on everyone. She was that special. It hadn't hurt that his mother had helped Judith start her own business, McAllister's Maids, and she became the first customer and a heavy advocate. The business had grown quickly, and now Becky's mother only managed it, with a whole staff who did the actual cleaning.

Watching his parents with Byron had been an even bigger shock. They might not have been good parents, but they did their best to make up for it as grandparents. And, of course, Byron loved having more family dote on him. The only one missing was Jack. Hopefully, one day Jack would grow up. But for now, nothing had changed. He'd gone from spoiled child to spoiled adult, but the one thing he hadn't counted on was his own mother finally saying enough.

His parents agreed tough love was in order, and they'd cut him off, wanting him to fend for himself, hoping he'd figure out how to be a better adult and get his act together.

"Byron, can we talk to you for a minute? We've got something to show and tell you."

"I love show and tell at school." He grinned.

"This should be just as good or better." Steve ruffled the boy's hair then squatted next to him. "You are, now and forever, my son."

"We got the adoption papers today."

"Yay! I love you, Daddy." Byron threw his arms around Steve and hugged him tight.

"I love you, too." Steve's vision blurred as his eyes watered, the emotions of the moment almost more than he could imagine. Byron was truly no longer his stepson or his nephew—he was his son. Steve's heart felt like it would burst with happiness.

"You said show and tell. What do you have to show me?" The kid didn't miss a thing.

"I've got that part covered." Becky smiled before returning to the house.

"Where's she going?" Byron asked, watching his mother walk away. "How can she show me something if she's leaving?"

"You'll see." Steve knelt next to Byron and waited for his wife to return with his son's present.

Minutes later, Becky came out the back door, holding the ten-week-old, mixed-breed puppy they'd picked out at the shelter. The golden retriever in the dog was a given considering the light reddish-golden fur and face, and they'd known right away the puppy would be an excellent pet for Byron.

"You got me a dog?" Byron ran to his mother's side, his smile as wide as the moon. "He's so sweet. Can I hold him? Can I?" he pleaded.

"If you sit down first, and then you need to be very gentle. And it's a she," Becky answered.

"Cool." Byron sat down in the grass and held out his hands. "I've always wanted a dog."

"Now that we have a house with lots of room for a dog to run and play, I thought it was a good idea for you to learn responsibility. You're getting to be such a big boy now." Becky placed the squirming puppy in his arms, guiding his hands to show him how to hold her correctly.

"Thanks, Mom. Thanks, Mr. St...Dad."

Steve loved the sound of the word. *Dad.*

"What are you going to name her?" Steve sat down next to him in the grass to pet the puppy.

"Goldilocks." Byron didn't hesitate with his answer. It was the special story he never tired of hearing, Steve style.

"That's a perfect name, son. You know, you two share a special bond."

"What's that?"

"I adopted you, and this puppy was adopted from a local shelter."

Becky smiled, watching the two of them together.

"Cool. We're going to be best friends forever." Byron beamed.

The dog struggled to get down. "It's okay to let her go. We just need to stay close by while she explores." Steve helped Byron to his feet, and hand in hand, they followed Goldilocks as she walked around the back yard, sniffing the scents of her new home, as Becky watched from the sidelines. They had another surprise for Byron, but they'd wait a few more months to let him know he would soon have a baby sister to play with as well.

***

If you enjoyed this sweet and charming romance, be sure to check out the
ALSO BY ELSIE DAVIS section on the next page for more clean and wholesome romance.

Want to keep in touch with new releases and what's happening in the world of Elsie Davis?
Sign up for the monthly newsletter at Elsie Davis.com

The greatest compliment you could give an author is to leave a review in order to help other readers discover the same great stories you enjoyed. Amazon/Bookbub/Goodreads are all great places. Many thanks!!! Another great way to keep in touch - ***Follow Elsie Davis on FaceBook***

Also By Elsie Davis

Sweet, Clean and Wholesome Stories...with a Happily-Ever-After Guarantee!

Great Smoky Mountain Getaways
(Christian Inspirational – Women's Fiction Romances)
Juliet's Journey to Love
Poppy's Path to Love
Rachel's Road to Love
Taylor's Trek to Love
Grace's Getaway to Love – 2024
Dixie's Detour to Love – 2025
Angel's Adventure to Love – 2025

Crossroads Creek Cowboys
(Christian Inspirational Romances)
The Heart of a Cowboy
The Help of a Cowboy
The Return of a Cowboy
The Care of a Cowboy
The Dream of a Cowboy – 2024

The Life of a Cowboy – 2025
The Tears of a Cowboy – 2025

Holidays in Hallbrook
(Sweet Romance Series for Holidays Throughout the Year)
Welcome to Hallbrook, New Hampshire. A small-town filled with the unexpected, lots of love, and of course, a beloved dog to ramp up the excitement.
Love & Order (Labor Day)
Love & Family (Thanksgiving)
Love & Peace (Christmas)
Love & Chocolate (Valentine's Day)
Love & Hope (Mother's Day)
Love & Liberty (Independence Day)
Love & Honor (Veteran's Day)
Love & Joy (Easter)
Love & Adventure (Father's Day)
Lov & Cheer (New Year's Day – TBD)

Crestfield Inn Romances
If you like special kinds of soulmates, a splash of the supernatural, and wholesome relationships, you'll adore this sweet bit of fun filled with romance and mystery.
Turning Back Time
Turning Up Roses
Turning Down Pie

Celebrity Corgi Romance
(Standalone Sweet Romance)
If you like light mystery mixed in with your happily-ever-after, you'll enjoy this second-chance romance and the race to save an adorable Corgi.
Digging the Driver

Gold Coast Retrievers
(Sweet Romance)
Special Golden Retrievers help their humans solve mysteries, save lives, and even find love...
Defending Dakota

Trinity River
(Sweet Western Romance)
Ranchers and farmers depend on the Trinity River for water, but when a secret conglomerate starts buying up property by fair means or foul, it's time for the landowners of Tumble County to fight back—Texas style. But what they don't count on, is finding love in the process.
Back in the Rancher's Arms
Small Town, Big Secrets

Sundancer's Legacy – 9 Book series

Sundancer's Star – Available Now

Sundancer's Joy – 2024

Sundancer's Heart – 2024 (2025)
2025/2026
Sundancer's Majesty
Sundancer's Miracle
Sundancer's Glory
Sundancer's Kiss
Sundancer's Moon
Sundancer's Splendor

About The Author

Elsie Davis is a *USA Today and International Best-selling Author* of over 30 sweet, clean, and wholesome romances, and a member of the ACFW. She discovered the world of Happily-Ever-After romance at the age of twelve when she began avidly reading Barbara Cartland, the Queen of Romance, and has been hooked ever since. After building her dream log home on top of a small mountain, she turned her attention to do what she loves most, writing. Elsie writes sweet Contemporary Romance and Contemporary Christian Romance from her heart...hoping to share a little love in a big world.

When she's not writing, she can be found birding, kayaking, camping, fishing, playing disc golf, and taking nature walks—hoping to spot wildlife. Basically, she loves all things outdoors, EXCEPT cold weather. She and her husband are avid Caribbean cruisers, but Elsie's favorite vacation was their cruise to Alaska. (In spite of the cold!) Indoors, she enjoys a toasty fire, and of course, a great romance with a guaranteed Happily-Ever-After.

https://www.elsiedavishea.com

www.ingramcontent.com/pod-product-compliance
Lightning Source LLC
Chambersburg PA
CBHW061736310726
48969CB00002BA/514